SINFUL LOVE

FINDING LOVE IN THE WRONGEST OF PLACES

RICHARD SCHREIBER

PLAY IT SAM PRESS

Reclaimer: Sinful Love: Finding Love in the Wrongest of Places © Copyright 2021 by Richard Schreiber

Copyright notice: All rights reserved under the International and Pan-American Copyright Conventions.

No part of this book may be reproduced or transmitted in any form or by any means, electronic or mechanical, including photocopying and recording, or by any information storage and retrieval system, without permission in writing from publisher.

This is a work of fiction. Names, places, characters, and incidents are either the product of the author's imagination or are used fictitiously, and any resemblance to any actual persons, living or dead, organizations, events, or locales is entirely coincidental.

Warning: the unauthorized reproduction or distribution of this copyrighted work is illegal. Criminal copyright infringement, including infringement without monetary gain, is investigated by the FBI and is punishable by up to 5 years in prison and a fine of $250,000.

For more information, email Richard.schreiber@gamil.com.

Content Warning: bad language and some sexually explicit scenes

Edited by: Pamela Elise Harris
Cover Design by: Diana Buidoso
Formatting by: Nola Li Barr

Print ISBN: 979-8-732-0-3450

THE KING OF HARLEM

The market crashes on that fateful day in October 1987, and Richard Frederick Graf's world tumbles into total chaos. He is a young, highly successful Wall Street stockbroker now without a job, and his apartment, car, everything he owned have now gone up in smoke, soon to be collateral damage. He has used up his savings fast. He is desperate.

Richard gets a phone call and hears a familiar voice. It is James Simpson, Richard's old friend and business confidant when they worked together at the messenger service a few years back. Richard and Simpson also spend many a night together carousing in Harlem bars near where James lived. They are also talking about going into business together.

Simpson swears to Richard he will come at him someday with a business proposition he cannot say not to. Is now that time?

His old friend makes Richard an offer Richard could not refuse— heading up the finance team at his organization offering a large off-the-books salary and a piece of the action, which the owner characterized as "a distribution business."

Richard just cannot pass this up, even though he knows in his heart there is something that seems not quite right about this business. It sounds too good to be true, but he is a bit naïve and signs on, in spite of a stern warning from his best friend, Brian Lowenstein, who advises him not to do anything desperate and stupid.

Over two years later, he is running the finances for the biggest crack operation in Manhattan for his friend James Simpson, laundering money, and he has created his own seven-digit offshore money stockpile. Nobody is allowed to leave the premises, which is known as the Crack Den, holed up in a large four building apartment or quad complex in Harlem. The crack operation occupies the entire fifteenth floor of the quad-buildings, terrorizing the remaining tenants to obtain their silence. This bothers Richard, but he is powerless to do anything about it.

Richard continues his mastery of overseeing the books, as well as all investments for the Crack Den's entire business. He continues to rake up high double-digit returns in the months that follow. He is assisted by a junior accountant who Richard additionally recruited from his days at Salomon Brothers, along with a team of two junior advisors/analysts he also recruited from his former Wall Street contacts. Richard runs the entire enterprise's finances, which have grown to hundreds of millions of dollars in holdings over the past two years, and he maintains Simpson's exclusive ear, as well as his trust.

Richard has direct oversight of everyone on the Den's finance team and provides financial advising for practically all of the Posse Men, who serve as James Simpson's security and enforcers, as well as the other employees at the Crack Den in exchange for favors and protection. Posse Men also served as Richard's escorts when he went to visit his mother or family.

James Simpson sees the opportunity to deal crack cocaine on an incredibly grand scale when its use is about to explode in the mid- to late-1980s, overwhelming law enforcement and enabling highly organized dealers to make huge sums of money off the addictive drug, those who can set up huge operations to create the drug and distribute it. Modeling their business after the mafia, a handful of high-end drug dealers, Simpson among them, hit real pay dirt in the late 1980s and early 1990s. As New York City is focused on ending the five mafia crime families, the drug lords fly under the radar for a time.

"Yo, I'm the king of Harlem!" Simpson bellows to all who will listen.

The setup he has established in the wayward Harlem apartment complex has separate living quarters for each "resident" worker bee, who processes and packs the product, and the "posse," the security/management and/or the advisory team. It is a finely tuned ecosystem and organization, ruled by fear and violence. Each worker resides in a shared room in an apartment, depending on the pecking order. Delivery personnel and individual dealers, often underaged teenage boys, come and go to and from the Den.

They occupy the entire top floor of the building, all twenty apartments on the fifteenth floor, having run the previous tenants on the floor out of their homes by threatening their lives. All except one eighty-year-old woman, Martha Flynn-Davis, who Simpson calls "Grandma" and he allows to live on their floor. Simpson has labelled her untouchable. Considering the way the rest of the tenants were expelled from the floor, it is an odd but telling part of Simpson's character, having been brought up by his grandmother when his mother died of breast cancer when he was four.

What the residents of the Den do inside their quarters is their business, but each unit is subject to periodic raids to ensure *no one* is consuming the product without permission. It is forbidden for workers to consume the product under fear of punishment, including the enforcers, the Posse Men, though it is not strictly enforced with them.

The loss of life is the ultimate penalty if one of them lets the drug get away from them. Posse men, however, distribute the drug frequently to the Home Girls to get them high, ensuring their ongoing addiction. Over the past two years, at least six workers responsible for cooking, cutting, and packing the crack vials were caught doing the drug and were executed in front of the entire workforce by Simpson's Posse henchmen to keep the troops in line.

This includes one worker that afternoon who is caught with a bag of vials in his pocket that he plans to smoke on his own.

"Die, you crackhead mothafucka!" screams enforcer HoJo Brown who drags the worker in front of the rest of the workforce.

Simpson was not prone to acts of violence himself, but in this case, he shoots the worker twice in the head and spits on the limp body on the floor in the large room where the drugs are packed up and prepared for sale as he walks away. He winks at Richard, standing nearby.

Simpson whispers the line from the 1970s TV show *Barretta*, "If you can't do the time, don't do the crime. Yo, Mookie, clean this up here, a'ight?"

The posse's leader, Mookie, is a ruthless but articulate black man, well trained in torture and martial arts. Two of his lead goons are former college football players. They work out onsite constantly and are nicknamed Curly and Big Flame. Mookie beckons them to remove the body and to call one of the porters employed by the den to clean up.

Richard and Mookie share a liking for basketball and are Knicks fans. Richard also gives Mookie stock tips and investment advice and helps grow Mookie's portfolio by multiples.

"You were right on shorting Apple. They're going down!" says Mookie to Richard, high fiving.

~

TWO YEARS LATER, it is now late December 1990. Richard and Simpson are talking in Simpson's office, sharing a cigar, and knocking down some fish and chips together.

"James, how long were you in business before I came on board in the beginning of 1988?"

Simpson says, "For just under a year before you, actually. We were just getting our distribution chains, all the runners, cookers, packagers, all the crew finalized. And we were still selling the shit. But it was chaotic, man. I also had to weed out a bunch of runners that were stealing cash. Yeah, had to make an example out of them." He pantomimed shooting in the air with his fingers, only this time Richard suspected it was no pantomime!

"By the time you came on board, we were hemorrhaging money through a couple of untrustworthy accountants who were syphoning off money in addition to making some bad investments. That was when, I guess, you were still a hot shot on Wall Street. You could have saved me a lot of pain, man, if you didn't hold out on me! I had to put down two of those accounting mothafuckas. In fact, one just two days before I hired you. Mothafucka was hiding cash in his apartment. Do you fucking believe that? Dumb mothafucka. At least if you're going to try to steal my money, be smart about it. Offshore the shit. Skim where nobody's looking. Dumb shit. Let's just say I know all the tricks. I've seen everything. So, don't go trying shit," Simpson half-jokes to Richard.

Richard doesn't say anything at first, then, "Yeah, you really have to be careful who you trust, especially with the money. You want to be laundering the cash smart. Offshore it where no one can touch it. You want to use the Caymans. No questions asked, easy to get there, and no Coast Guard. Otherwise, a bunch of cash isn't worth anything. It doesn't seem like my predecessor knew that."

Richard now remembers the conversation with his close friend Brian Lowenstein, who he left behind when Richard left his entire life behind to join Simpson on his criminal enterprise. Lowenstein warned him about the job, as Richard described to him, being likely something that was not on the up and up. Richard is momentarily stopped by the pain of that memory, now caused by how things turned out. Simpson, noticing Richard is not present, snaps his fingers.

"Yo, I know you know a lot about laundering cash!" Simpson says.

"Well, I know you have to wash it through legitimate businesses, ultimately. But that's not our concern now. I have set us up as you know with a pipeline and connection with someone direct in the

Caymans where I send all the cash to. We drive it to Miami and then by boat to the Caymans, right into our own private bank," says Richard.

"Right, you told me," says Simpson. At times, even James Simpson marveled at his friend's financial savvy and that he quickly adapted from being a stockbroker to illicit money trafficking. "Where did you learn all of this? "

"On Wall Street. I had clients that I knew were laundering money. They would give me large cash deposits to invest. I didn't care about that. I never had an issue with where the money came from. But eventually I learned the ropes because my clients got me curious, and eventually they confided in me. Man, they laundered millions. I never dreamed I'd be putting what they taught me to use, James. I have you to blame for that!" He and James exchange a boisterous high five.

"Yeah, you and me, we are a killer team," says James.

"James, no woman in your life?" Richard asks out of the blue.

"Yo, Richard, you knew I was married back in the day. Don't you remember Rebecca? She was sweet. Smart girl. Went to Princeton. But this was no life for her. I left her behind, I set her up down in North Carolina with the kid. She's doing fine without me. We have an arrangement. Someday, maybe we'll pick up where we left off."

"Shit, you have a kid with her? What's his/her name? How old is he/she?"

"His name is Bostock. He's six. Smart boy."

Richard nods and says, "Yeah, this is certainly no life for family. I hope after we get rich, we can retire early, and you can get back with her."

"Yo, I'm a gangster now, man. Ain't no place for woman nor a kid!" Simpson bellows.

"A gangster? I thought you were always better than that," says Richard.

"Nothing wrong with being a gangster, long as the money comes in. Don't worry, I won't ask you to kill anyone, not with your pen or your computer keyboard!"

SINFUL LOVE

"That's funny, James. I can handle myself. You remember, I took martial arts when I was young. First degree black belt when I was fifteen. Though I'm a little rusty now."

"Yeah. Boards don't hit back!" says Simpson, a line from the Bruce Lee movie *Enter the Dragon* that they had watched together years back at a Greenwich Village cinema house in New York back in the day.

Just then, Mookie arrives. "James, we got a problem. The police are here. Got complaints from tenants about all the human traffic going in and out of the building, our runners. They say they are coming back with a warrant. Should I call Chief Flanagan?"

James's look sours. "Yeah, call that fuck. Tell him he needs to squash this. I don't have that mothafucka on the payroll for nothing. Find out who's making noise. These fucking tenants. I'll give them a little reminder to shut the fuck up and mind their manners."

"James, may I suggest maybe a different approach," begins Richard. "Instead of intimidating the tenants any further, why don't we make life easier for the tenants. Let's fix this dilapidated tenement building up a bit. Give people some new TVs, fix their places up, and kind of bring them into the fold, so they cooperate. If they got nothing to gripe about, they'll be more compliant, less likely to go to the cops. We make them, sort of, partners. We can't have law enforcement getting close to our operations."

Richard knows appealing to James out of humanity will not stick. He has to position it in a way that there is clear-cut benefit, especially financial one to James and the Den.

James thinks about it for a moment and says, "Maybe you're on to something, smart boy. Yeah, I like the sound of that. Let's come up with a plan. Get some of guys to survey the building with you, see what needs to be fixed, and then check up on the tenants and their apartments. Fix whatever needs fixing. A couple of our guys used to work construction. Make 'em know I'm really benevolent and shit. Fear and benevolence are a powerful combination! You are a renaissance man. Shit," he says in admiration. He once again high-fives Richard.

Richard says, "I'm fine to head this up. I did some renovations on my apartment when I bought it. I can reach out to some contractors I know and trust. They don't need to know anything. I can get Mookie and Roger to help with the tenants, meet with them, listen to them."

"Whatever you need. This is your baby. Make it happen. I'll get the guys behind this."

Richard is ecstatic that he is able to sell his plan to James. He knows in the long run it will reap benefits. But he especially likes that it will take the tenants out of the Den's crosshairs.

James, now out of the blue, says, "Yo, you should have some female companionship."

Richard says, "Not my number one priority right now, Smoke, but what do you have in mind?"

Simpson gets up from his seat to show Richard some pictures taken of women who were being indoctrinated as residents at the Den. "Check it out!"

Richard looks at the pictures. "They all look like fine women, James, but I'm really OK. I'm on a roll and don't want any distractions right now. I want to finish strong in these last six weeks of the year." Richard then gets a bit pensive.

"James, remember those times we used to go up to Harlem, to— What was the name of that place on One Hundred and Twenty-Fifth Street? The jazz bar, they used to have live music?"

"The 7 M&M. I remember that time you picked up that girl— What was her name? Michelle? Yeah, man she was hot. Nice brown eyes—from around there. I knew you would love uptown girls over those hangers-on you used to pick up at that place, Jeremy's downtown with your friend, your home boy—what was his name? Lowenstein? Bunch of one-night stands! You needed to meet a girl like Michelle. You were really into her. These black bitches go gaga for those baby blues you have! They really appreciate a dude like you who knows how to treat a woman all respectful and shit like you do, my friend."

"Yeah, Michelle was cute, really warm and fun, too. I really liked her. Too bad she moved to North Carolina later that year," says Richard. "I used to put on some Al Green or Staple Singers, Bill Withers, and we would slow dance at my apartment and then..." Richard's memories of very intimate scenes with Michelle stopped him. He really had strong feelings for Michelle.

"Yo, you need an outlet, bro. I'm afraid I'm not asking. You all need some work life balance and shit. Pick one of these now, bro, so I can set you up. You know, I remember you like 'em thin and athletic-like and shit."

The Den also maintains a group of women known as the Home Girls, who are typically young and attractive black or Hispanic women in their twenties. They serve essentially as Posse groupies, either for sex or companionship, not unlike a harem. They are considered a perk, and every Posse and management team member is encouraged to indulge, including Richard, though he has always chosen not to partake, except on one prior occasion. Was that about to change?

HAILEY ROSS

It is now a month later, January 1991. Three young African American women are spotted begging for crack cocaine on 128th Street and St. Nicholas Avenue from one of the Crack Den's young drug handlers, by Homer, a member of the Den posse. It is only two blocks away from the crack house the three have just recently left.

"Hey, why don't you come with me. I can promise you what you're looking for. Plus, we got some food, a place to stay. You'd like it," says Homer to the trio.

One of the girls, Nicole Watkins, is quick to say, "I'm down. Let's do this, girls!"

The other two girls, shrug in agreement.

"Where are we going?" asks Hailey Ross, another one of the girls, nervously.

"C'mon, Hailey, it'll be fun! They have shit waiting for us!"

Hailey hesitates for just a moment but then reluctantly agrees, " OK."

The three hop into a cab with the Posse Man for a short ride to the Den. Hailey Ross looks out of place because, in spite of being on drugs, she has maintained her appearance, still carrying her makeup purse in her hand.

SINFUL LOVE

Hailey stares out the taxi car window, not knowing what is to come, but tries to figure out how to get off this pointless drug-infested merry-go-round she's gotten herself onto.

Hailey remembers a different time, just a short year and a half ago before she ended up on the streets of Harlem high on crack cocaine.

A large college graduation ceremony occurs inside a huge auditorium decorated festively. It is June 1989, and Hailey Ross, a strikingly beautiful and petite young light-skinned black woman, is receiving her pre-law degree with honors from Temple University in Philadelphia. She looks stunning in the bright red cap and gown that are the Temple Owls colors. A crowd of several thousand sits comfortably on the red velvet seats in the auditorium, many with hand fans to battle the early summer Philadelphia heat.

Hailey's family and friends from her hometown of Atlanta are there. Her parents, both in their late fifties, sit beaming with pride, dressed as they say in the south, "all gussied up," their version of "to a T." Her mom's astonishing white hat styled in the southern look, big and wide with exquisite highlights, is a centerpiece for sure. Her parents both stand as Hailey receives her diploma on stage, and a roar goes out from her friends and family in the crowd.

There is a celebratory lunch with Hailey's entire family and friends at a well-known restaurant Le Bec Fin after the ceremony. It is an opulent jewel box of a restaurant with incredible French food. Much joy abounds.

At lunch, Hailey announces she has been accepted to Columbia Law School in Manhattan and will start in the fall. Her mom, an attorney, beams at the thought. Her dad, a Baptist minister of a large church in Atlanta, is equally proud. They toast to Hailey, and everybody is thrilled.

"And to Mom and Dad for believing in me and standing by me and for my education!" gushes Hailey in testament to her parents.

In conversation during lunch, Hailey says she has been to New York only on one occasion, when she checked Columbia Law School out, and is excited about the opportunity to attend law school there.

She adds, "In Philly, I didn't stray too far from the campus, I'm not sure how safe it was, but I am really excited about going to the Big Apple to explore the big city. It's going to be far more exciting than Philadelphia!"

Her parents are pleased as well because they know the importance of a law degree from a top Ivy League school—a sure-fire way to a top law firm, maybe in New York, post-graduation.

Her mom says with pride, "Hailey, honey, the world is yours for the taking. Go get New York!"

Hailey raises her wine glass in a toast.

It is an image she now longs for. She turns to the window and begins to cry softly.

∽

THEY ARRIVE at the Den and walk into the main lobby, where Hailey is further taken aback by the dilapidated look. They take the elevator upstairs to the fifteenth floor. Hailey and the other two girls are then shown their "accommodations" in a tiny one-bedroom apartment. It much more resembles squalor, at least four bunk beds spread out in the living room, messes of bottles, cartons, garbage strewn all over the room, the curtains drawn, and the room dark and smelling of drugs and alcohol.

Hailey goes and rests on the bed she's staked out, not moving. One of her roommates, a girl named Sasha, about the same age, black, attractive, but looking disheveled, says, "the doors don't lock here, honey. Them Posse Men just come here when they want and snatch us up," she said.

"Are you serious?" asks Hailey. "Oh, my God. This is inhuman."

Ron John, a Posse Man, standing by the door who overhears Hailey, chuckles, "You're right. That's why you need to hook up with, you know, one of us for protection and perks." Ron John sticks out his tongue in Hailey's direction, and she recoils.

Hailey shudders thinking what currency she has to provide in exchange for the protection and "perks." The other girls, Nicole and her friend, Denise, say nothing, seeming to be too preoccupied.

"Yo, I need a hit," barks Denise.

Ron John looks at her, laughs, and says, "Bitch, you need to be patient. You'll get your shit when we're good and ready. You just be ready to do yo part, ho."

Hearing that exchange sends chills down Hailey's back. She turns away from Ron John, physically disgusted.

Oh my God, what have I gotten myself into? she thinks. Her feeling of hopelessness is compounded. She takes a deep breath. Should she pray for a knight in shining armor? She had no idea her unlikely prince was about to cross her path.

FROM BLUES TO HAILEY

Over the past few months, James Simpson notices Richard has become increasingly sullen and sedentary and introspective after his tragic escapade the prior year with the former Home Girl Danielle. Danielle could not stop doing crack and had a heart attack from an overdose. Richard had found her dead on the floor in his apartment.

Richard has admitted his sadden funk to Simpson. So, at Simpson's behest, Richard agrees reluctantly to meet some of the new members of the Home Girls. James thinks it is time Richard put the experience with Danielle behind him and is convinced that female companionship will brighten Richard up. Simpson is concerned that his finance guru and friend shows little interest in anything else and may eventually crack. Richard claims he is not sad and is fine, just focused on doing the job, but Simpson knows better.

"Yo, you need to meet someone, Richard. Put a little spark in your step. Get your head back up," says James.

Richard nods.

Richard walks to the large foyer of the main apartment off the hallway. Among the Posse's new round of Home Girls, Richard spies an attractive petite and young light-skinned black woman from across the hallway.

SINFUL LOVE

One of the new recruits, he surmises.

Richard instantly notices her because of her striking beauty and because he senses she is different. She carries herself in a classier way and actually is wearing some makeup, trying to look presentable.

To Richard, she has obvious class and intelligence exuding from her in spite of her being in the Den. She is casually talking to one of the Posse Men now in Richard's earshot. She talks in slow measured, intelligent words. Richard notices how out of place she is. The woman is smart and articulate!

Richard continues to eye her from a distance where the Posse Men gather. Richard overhears Hailey mention to one of the Posse Men, LeRoy, with total clarity and in a well-spoken manner how she is in law school and how as an undergraduate she finished second from the top of her class. LeRoy is unimpressed, but Richard is. He is immediately drawn to her.

"Bitch, you not in law school anymore," said LeRoy.

Richard does not make eye contact with her, though he keeps asking himself, *what is she doing here?*

She looks so out of place for sure, he thinks. Most of the girls that come to the Den strung out on crack are less sophisticated or educated and certainly less physically attractive than Hailey.

Richard leaves to go back to his duties, checking each offshore account carefully for any red flags. Later, after dinner, he meets James Simpson in his office to talk about the day's proceeds and to shoot the breeze.

Richard over the years has worked long hours setting up the accounting practices and investments for Simpson and is often rewarded with perks and privileges, such as tickets to professional ballgames, always escorted, usually by Posse Man leader Mookie, also a big sports fan. After all, he was nicknamed after Mets outfielder Mookie Wilson.

Simpson says, "I heard you were eyeing that pretty young thing we brought in today. I understand she says she graduated top two of her class from Temple or some shit. What the fuck is she doing here?

Anyway, I thought you two should meet. Be good for you. She's obviously someone smart and shit. She'd be right for you. You like them smart ones, light-skinned ones."

Richard says, "Light-skinned ones? You got me pegged? Yeah, she's really pretty and smart and clearly a fish out water here. Oh, I don't know, Smoke. Danielle was hard for me to get over. I just don't really want to be involved right now."

"Bullshit," shot back Simpson. "Yo, I told you earlier, if she's the one, you can clean her up, maybe have her to yo' self. I need your 'A' game, man."

"Seriously, James. How can they get and stay clean with the drugs everywhere in their rooms being handed out like candy by the Posse Men?"

"Yo, don't worry about that. Yo, you're my homes. I want you to be happy, man," says Simpson.

In an unusual gesture, Simpson summons Hailey to introduce her to Richard. Mookie escorts her to Simpson's office and faces her in front of Simpson at his desk.

"Hailey, your name is? Benny told me your name. Anyway, this here is my right hand, my best friend, Richard Graf. You can trust those baby blues. He's the main man around here, after me. Say hello," says Simpson.

Richard almost blushes from the intro and manages a weak smile at Hailey. He stretches out his hand to Hailey and says "hello." Hailey replies with a "hello" and takes Richard's hand without making eye contact. Hailey does not look as disheveled as the other women and in fact, Richard notices she still carries what looks like a makeup bag with her, odd to him that she would bring it with her to Simpson's office. Richard observes right off the bat that Hailey is uncomfortable about her surroundings.

Simpson encourages the two of them to get comfortable in his office. "Take my office. Have a drink, a conversation, and get to know one another. Help yourself to the bar cart back there," he says, motioning to the bar cart behind his desk stocked with various alcohol bottles.

"Hailey, Richard is as solid a dude as you'll ever find...for a white guy." Simpson laughs heartily as he leaves the office. "Just leave it the way you found it."

Richard clears his throat and says, "How are you? I know you probably didn't come here willingly. They told me you had a couple of friends with you. I hope they're all right."

Hailey says nothing. She is still numbed by her surroundings and actually quite afraid and not sure why this guy knows so much about her and why he tries to seem concerned.

Richard continues, "It's OK. Why don't you sit down for a moment? Maybe you can tell me a little about yourself. It's OK. Really, I won't bite."

Hailey looks at Richard with a weak smile. "It's OK?" she says under her breath. *Who are you fucking kidding?* she thinks, wondering why this guy seems so friendly.

Richard continues, as he sits in one of the chairs in front of Simpson's desk, "I'm originally from New York. I was born in Astoria, Queens. My family is from Germany originally. I studied finance. I was a stockbroker. I was doing great until Black Monday. Then I lost it all."

Richard immediately sees Hailey is quiet. With her refusal to make eye contact or even acknowledge him, he deduces she is probably not interested in his story. Hailey continues to stand awkwardly next to Richard.

"I'm sorry. It's all right if you don't want to talk. I'm babbling away. I don't want you to feel uncomfortable. Why don't you sit down," says Richard.

Hailey has a faint smile and looks up Richard for the first time, making eye contact. Unaccustomed to seeing many men with piercing blue eyes, Hailey stares right into his eyes for a long time. Richard smiles broadly and stares back. He is transfixed. A playful feeling momentarily comes over Hailey. She senses an innocence in Richard's eyes that seem absent in everyone else she has met in the Den. She actually senses his vulnerability, and she softens.

Hailey smiles and finally introduces herself with a simple, "Hi, I'm Hailey. Nice to meet you." She takes his hand again while never breaking eye contact.

Richard is ecstatic that he finally got Hailey to speak. They continue to stare into each other's eyes.

The fact Richard does not break eye contact surprises Hailey. *He wants to let me in*, she thinks.

Richard feels chills go up his spine, and his whole-body tingles as he has never felt such a connection with such a beautiful woman nor experienced such intimate contact without touch. He instantly feels warm inside. It is a mesmerizing moment for him, though for a moment he wonders if it is the drug ramping up her interest. Or is it? He does not think so.

Hailey sees something in Richard's eyes that reassures her. She finally opens up.

"I'm...I'm from Atlanta. My mom's a lawyer. My dad is a Baptist pastor," Hailey begins, no longer making eye contact with Richard. "I went to school at Temple. Graduated at the top of my class." Hailey fidgets a bit, likely from the drugs, "I was in law school at Columbia when things just got out of control."

She starts to cry softly. Richard gets up as if to comfort her, but Hailey motions for him not to approach her and to sit back down. Richard reluctantly sits down in one of the chairs in front of James's desk. Hailey composes herself and finally sits down next to Richard in the other chair and turns toward him.

"Hailey, I'm so sorry you ended up here. But I'm glad to meet you. I'd...I'd like to be your friend if that's OK," says Richard, immediately realizing how awkward and forward that sounded.

"I'd like that," Hailey says indifferently, though the thought of having a friend in her current circumstances really resonated with her. "Richard, what is it like here? It...it looks really scary to me. They have us in rooms that don't lock, bunking up—"

SINFUL LOVE

"I really don't know, Hailey. I've kind of been just functioning on my job here the last year or so, not really paying attention to anything else. You can't really go anywhere here. I know there are some things I want to change around here, like the mistreatment of the tenants."

Hailey nods. "And of the girls, too."

Richard grimaces. "Yes, I've heard that too," he says softly. "Hailey, would you like to take a walk? There's a really nice view from apartment 15X at the end of the hall. It even has a balcony. I like to go there sometimes at the end of the day just to watch the sunset. It's the only apartment that doesn't have the curtains all drawn or the windows boarded up because there's nothing with the business that goes on here. It's sort of our escape if you will, to the outside world, albeit from a distance."

"OK," says Hailey. She fidgets again as she is really feeling withdrawal symptoms from the drug. Richard notices and offers his arm to Hailey to help her up off the chair. Hailey takes his arm, and they both get up from their respective chairs and walk out of Simpson's office. Richard leads, making sure to give Hailey some space and he walks slowly. Hailey walks close to Richard at one point brushing his hand, though she does not take it. Richard notices and smiles.

They reach the balcony. It is close to sunset. Richard says, "It's a nice night, isn't it? I love the view from here. Should be a beautiful sunset in a little while. Temple, eh? How did you like Philly?"

But just as Richard starts to move closer to Hailey, HoJo, a large black and surly member of the Posse, overhearing their voices, walks into the balcony pushes Richard aside, and steps in between them. Richard is tall and fit, but HoJo is much larger and definitely stronger. He is not one of the Posse Men Richard has befriended because he is a rank sociopath.

Richard decides to play it cool...for now and backs off, saying, "HoJo. We were just talking. What is it you need?"

"I don't need anything from yo punk ass, bitch. Hey, Hay-lee! Damn, you fine, girl! Why ain't you partyin' with the Posse now at the room? We got weed and some of the illest crack in Harlem!" HoJo bellows, as if that's some kind of incentive. HoJo grabs Hailey by the arm and starts to stalk back into the apartment.

Richard follows them, saying, "HoJo, wait." HoJo stops and turns back toward Richard.

Hailey is forced to smile at HoJo's aggressive charm. "Well, Mr. Simpson had just introduced me to Richard here, so I was saying hello."

HoJo cocks his head at an angle and looks at Richard. "Well, you met our accountant. He can do your taxes if you like. While he gets down to his business, let's you and me get down to our *business*!" HoJo quickly puts his lips and tongue to Haley's face. She squirms in disgust.

Richard instinctively puts his arm between HoJo and Hailey. Richard says, "That's enough!"

HoJo shoves Richard to the ground. HoJo smirks and takes out his gun waving it menacingly at Richard. "Only Posse Men are allowed to hold one of these. Are you a Posse Man, Mr. Accountant?"

Richard is stunned, but he stares straight and coolly at HoJo and the barrel of his gun. Richard slowly rises up and pushes HoJo's gun out of his face with a swift move. For a split second, his martial arts instincts from his youth kick in, but he decides not to go farther there.

"By the way, I'm not the accountant. I'm the CFO. That's Chief Financial Officer. And I'm untouchable, HoJo, you meathead. Plus, if you had any money or inclination to invest, I could make that grow for you. But then again, you seem happy with what you have, or should I say what you don't have, eh, HoJo?" Richard replies.

The commotion on the balcony has caught the ear of some nearby traffic. HoJo is angry at what Richard has just said and is about to get in Richard's face. "You mothafucka, smart boy," he says moving toward Richard.

Richard has gotten into a defensive karate stance that temporarily confuses HoJo.

Right then, one of the Home Girls, Anita, comes toward HoJo, clearly intoxicated.

SINFUL LOVE

"Hey, man," she says. "Are we gettin' this party on, or are we just fucking around? You promised weed, mothafucka!" This clearly cuts the tension in the room.

"I'm on it," HoJo says, chuckling. "I'm bringing *all* my good shit to *this* party. All my good shit!"

Just like that, HoJo grabs Hailey with his free hand, dragging her through the apartment, down the hallway and toward his room while waving his gun. The Home Girl, anxious for her next hit of anything and oblivious to the danger, follows them. Richard follows them for a stretch, but then turns away in resignation, powerless to go after Hailey and HoJo. So much for first impressions. He relaxes from his karate stance, realizing he was shaking, probably because he was a little rusty as it's been years since he's done karate competitively.

He heads back to his office in Apartment 15A and pretends as if the interlude never happened.

Still, the relatively brief encounter with Hailey has left a mark on Richard as he is really intrigued by her. When their eyes met and lingered, he felt a real spark he had never felt before. He is also angry at HoJo's Neanderthal behavior and mad at himself for his inability to do anything about his newfound interest being whisked away from him like a pet with HoJo brandishing a gun.

While HoJo is an animal, he is a key figure and enforcer in the Posse Men, and he has James's ear and protection. It is the first time Richard is really dealing with the consequences of his surroundings at the Den personally, and it makes him angry, especially this time because he felt powerless.

In his mind, he sees himself taking HoJo out next time but cannot risk it as long as HoJo has a gun. It is an image and a feeling that sticks with him as he promises himself next time, it will be different, and he will not back down. A dangerous promise in these surroundings. Still, he seems suddenly alive again after his time with Hailey. He wants more. Something has shifted inside him. Could he too be finally waking from his moral slumber?

POSSE MEN

The Posse Men appear to befriend the Home Girls, introducing them to a happening scene offering good times, drugs, and male companionship. Some of the Posse Men offer the girls limited quantities of crack to elicit the most starved sexual activity out of them to keep them essentially as their sex slaves, often abusing, demeaning, and mistreating them.

Home Girls have their own squalor-like accommodations where they bunk two or more to a room in barrack-like conditions in the smaller one-bedroom apartments, and the unlocked doors again enable the Posse Men to intrude on them at will. It is a frightful experience as at any time one of the girls can be pulled out of the rooms and forced to have sex with a Posse Man after getting high with them. It is especially hard on Hailey as she has never experienced anything like this before. She does her best to avoid Posse Men.

Posse members often have Home Girls visit them in their own private quarters, which are the nicer apartments in the complex. But because Home Girls are crack addicts, Posse members have to constantly watch everything they own for fear they will steal anything they can get their hands on to barter to get more crack.

"Bitch let me see yo pockets. Empty them now," can be heard constantly from Posse Men confronting the girls. Discovery of property belonging to a Posse Man from their pockets will invariably result in a hard slap or worse on the girl. HoJo has been known to break bones and bloody girls who unwisely attempted to take something from him.

Home Girls are often "traded" back and forth by the various Posse Men as currency, and Posse Men never develop any serious relationship with any single girl. That makes it easier to justify their demeaning treatment of them. They consider them whores and treat them as such. Simpson only generally enforces orders that any abuse not get out of hand or be considered what is criminally violent, such as striking the women causing them to be bloody or bruised. Simpson has on occasion reprimanded a Posse Man in front of the rest but not HoJo, his main enforcer.

Richard makes his disdain for HoJo in particular's treatment of women *quite clear*. In a meeting with Simpson and HoJo later that afternoon in Simpson's office, Richard says, "HoJo, can't you just treat the women with a little respect? Bad enough you force yourself on them all the time. Do you really need to beat on them?"

HoJo snarls back at Richard, "Bitch, I'll fuck you up."

Richard stares HoJo down as if ready to fight. HoJo stares right back. They are only a few feet apart. Richard feels emboldened.

Richard has not yet told Simpson of the outcome of his introduction to Hailey and how HoJo literally grabbed and dragged Hailey away at gunpoint from him in spite of Richard's protest.

Simpson looks up for a moment at HoJo and says, "Yo, HoJo, don't beat on the hos. We need them to keep the rest of the crew happy, you understand?" Simpson's look at HoJo is steely. "Yo, HoJo, Richard says a couple of the pickup points are light, these two in Morningside Heights. I want you to go down there and fix this, you dig? That's it. Dismissed."

HoJo nods.

HoJo turns away from Simpson to face Richard and sneers at him under his breath, "just let me get you outside of this room, punk. I'll kill you."

Richard overhears and looks HoJo in the eye and whispers back, "Big, tough guy beating on women. Don't forget who I work for jackass. You want me? You know where I am. Come and get me."

HoJo waves a finger at Richard and pantomimes his index finger as a gun and pretends to shoot Richard and then walks out of Simpson's office.

Simpson without looking up, says to Richard, "What's going on between you two? I would steer clear of HoJo. He's like that Wookiee character in *Star Wars*. HoJo's been known to pull people's arms out of their socket if you cross him. Plus, I'd hate to have to put him down, just to save your ass, you dig? He serves an important purpose around here. He's my main collector. So, give him space, you hear?"

Richard replies, "I'm not interested in making any trouble with him. But he does need to dial back the violence to the women. He's also threatened me. If he comes after me, I'm going to defend myself, James. I'll take him out. His violence can draw attention to us, especially if he's beating up women and the word gets out to law enforcement. People in the building do talk." Richard still cannot get himself to talk to James about the humiliating scene with him, Hailey, and HoJo.

Simpson says, "You let *me* worry about that. Now, how's the books today? Where are we?"

"We're right on target. There are a couple of other distribution points running a little behind. Drew and Smiley. June Bug, too. Yesterday's take was six hundred four thousand dollars. Investments are up 20.5 percent this month. A few hunches I played really paid off."

Simpson looks up. "You're the best. Remember five percent of that off the top is yours. Go play. I'll let HoJo speak to these other delinquent connects when he gets back."

"Delinquent?" asks Richard.

"Yeah, we got a couple of connects up in Washington Heights that have been coming up short, too. I'm aware of it. You didn't notice because the cash was on target. But they've been siphoning cash, skimming. But you don't need to worry about that. HoJo's just the man or that job."

Richard walks out, smiling. For once he is relieved, he's not going to be on the receiving end of HoJo's violence. His five percent take on the business's profits since his arrival has already, with his own investment schemes, netted Richard close to three million dollars. He has stashed it in his own offshore account. Richard and his accounting team keep copious records, and they are aware of the five percent diversion, which Richard explains to the rest of the team is a "rainy day fund" that only Richard controls.

Little do they know it is being syphoned off into his own offshore account that is untraceable, even to them.

Suddenly he has forgotten all about Hailey. And HoJo. Still, Hailey has left a mark on him, and he cannot get her entirely out of his mind. She is so diminutive, perfect for him to wrap his arms around her and cuddle with her. He sees her face, their eyes locking in his mind. It stops him for a moment. He composes himself. He wonders when he will see her again. Then, it struck him. He has access like no one in the den. He can find Hailey if he really wants to. A smile comes over his face. He controls his destiny more than most at the Den.

A CHANCE MEETING

Hailey and Richard have a chance second meeting two days later, as Richard is leaving a meeting with the boss.

Richard and James had been reminiscing their initial meeting when James Simpson offered Richard the job as CFO at the Crack Den over two years ago.

Richard recalled that he was initially scared as he was escorted from the lobby of the Harlem apartment complex up to James's office by one of the menacing Posse Men on that winter morning in 1988. But Simpson greeted him warmly that day. Richard starts daydreaming about his exchange with James back then:

"Good to see you, man. I told you we would do some business one day. Remember those days when we were working at the messenger service over on Fifty-Fifth Street? Shit, you used to send me all over the city as a messenger. We talked about this, one day, we'd be doing business together, and now it's here!"

Richard nods and says evenly, "Good to see you, too. What kind of business are you in?"

Simpson says, "Let's just say I'm an entrepreneur in the distribution business. I give people what they want. I keep people happy.

SINFUL LOVE

Richard, what I'm about to tell you doesn't leave this room, understand?"

Richard, puzzled, nods, and agrees. He notices James has an intense expression that Richard has not really seen before, but he infers it to mean business. Richard still has not changed his lack of expression.

Simpson continues, "You've heard of crack cocaine, right?"

Richard shakes his head. He has not.

"Well, it has become the biggest thing, my friend. It's the jammie! People go crazy over this shit! Bitches will do anything for a hit of it in these glass pipes and shit. They become like zombie sex slaves. They'll give it up in a heartbeat for more of this shit. And everybody is into this shit, Wall Street types, lawyers, doctors, everybody, white, black, Chinese, I mean everybody!"

"We have the largest crack operation in Manhattan right here. We control this whole apartment complex. We deal the shit all over the five boroughs from our HQ right here, man. We have serious market share and growing. We have the best shit out there, too. Call it Midnight Blue 'cause the bottle tops the crack comes in are a custom color, midnight blue. We have a direct pipeline to Miami, man. Shit coming in right off the mother fucking boat!"

Richard acknowledges his friend's passion and energy. "Wow, James, I can see you're really into this. Well, I hope I can make a difference for you," almost cringing because of how corporate he sounds.

Simpson continued, putting his arm around Richard, "I need someone I can trust to do the books, to set up my investments, and to run the finances for my business. I'll pay you two hundred and fifty thousand dollars a year in cash. You can invest it however you like. I'll give you a bonus based on how you invest our capital. You get to keep two points over ten percent in return, four points if we hit twenty percent. How's that? Yo, you won't have any expenses, so you pocket the cash clean, understand, bro?"

Richard nods, takes a deep breath, and says, "Also, whatever I make on the side, like extra, by helping anyone on your team invest, is mine also. You know I like to spread it around, help everyone I come in contact with to invest smartly in their future. OK? Also, I get to see my Mom when I need to, even if it's with one of your Posse Men escorts. Otherwise, I'm in."

Simpson shrugs and exclaims, "Now, that's what I'm talking about! You start right now." They shake hands and embrace. Simpson smiles at his old friend.

Richard then recalls, again, talking with his best friend Brian Lowenstein, who had to sublet his apartment as Richard moved into the Den, with limited access to the outside world.

"Dude," says Lowenstein, "What kind of gig is this, man? Sounds really mysterious if you have like one day to make everything happen and then you'll be like a prisoner there."

Richard suddenly snaps out of his daydream, back to the present and now spots Hailey walking toward him outside Simpson's office in the main apartment, Apartment A. He is surprised to see Hailey and greets her warmly, "Hi, Hailey. Nice to see you again."

But now she is far more reserved. She even avoids eye contact with him.

Richard asks, "What are you doing in the office? Well anyway, I'm glad to see you. Would you like to take a walk together?"

Hailey says nothing, looking away from Richard. But she does walk next to him. They walk together in silence out of the main apartment into the elevator lobby area.

Richard keeps chatting with Hailey pleasantly. "Where have you been the last couple of days? I haven't seen you, and I was hoping we could finish our conversation."

She again is guarded. Then, as if angered by Richard's nonchalance, she says, "What the hell do you think I've been doing? Playing pinochle? I've been trying to stay alive and keep away from the Posse Men and getting high."

SINFUL LOVE

That gets Richard's attention as to him Hailey's reaction is completely unexpected. "Whoa. What happened? Please tell me. I want to know, Hailey."

Hailey again says nothing. Richard is distressed that Hailey has become a bit hostile toward him, and he is not sure how to react. He wants to draw her out though and thinks to himself about disrupting the current situation.

"Hey, let's get out of here. We can sit outside in the courtyard downstairs, if you like. They let me do that. Come on. I'm sorry. I didn't mean to upset you. The fresh air sometimes does us good," says Richard.

"Richard, what do you think happens to the women around here? Don't you have your eyes wide open? Are you that freaking naïve?" Hailey fights back tears in anger. She also begins to realize her anger directed at Richard may not be fair because he really seems clueless about what goes on. She just cannot understand why he would not know.

He must be in some kind of bubble, she thinks.

Richard turns away and again mumbles, "I'm so sorry. Yes, I know it has to be pretty awful. I've heard some of the Posse Men are kind of wild. I want to change that. I told James the girls are being mistreated and it has to stop—"

Hailey cuts him off, "OK. Let's walk. The courtyard sounds nice." She chides herself again for being so curt with Richard. She looks at him with a faint smile as if to say it is OK.

"Sure, Hailey, you can tell me what happened. Really, I want to know," says Richard in earnest.

They get in the elevator, Richard tells the Posse Man Karl, standing guard outside the elevator, "We're just going to the courtyard for a stretch to get some air. James says it's OK."

The Posse Man motions Richard into the elevator. Hailey is impressed that Richard gets no questions asked. They walk out outside into the vast courtyard that is in the middle of the apartment complex, and Hailey awkwardly follows. There are several Posse Men patrolling. They notice Richard and nod.

Hailey sits uncomfortably next to Richard on a park bench in the middle of the courtyard. She says, "Seems you've got a lot of pull around here. You can come and go as you please. No one else can. What's up with that?"

"I manage all the finances here. I help most of those guys invest their money. It keeps them on my side. I'm also a good friend of James's. I'm his right-hand man I guess you could say."

"Smart. Good friends with the crack lord. I'm impressed," says Hailey with a hint of sarcasm.

The words sting Richard a little, as he looks away. Hailey notices and wonders where Richard stands in all of this.

Richard is frustrated that whatever he seems to say in his view gains Hailey's ire. "Yeah, you're right. But James wasn't always a drug kingpin. We go way back. We used to work together when I was going to undergraduate school. I was always impressed by his business sense even though I know he just had a couple of years at a community college in North Carolina, I think it was. We always talked about opening a business together, making a fortune together. I never imagined it would be like this."

Richard frowns. "But I'm like a captive here. I barely get to see my mother and family. They only let me out once in a while and always with an escort with one of the Posse Men." Suddenly, it struck Richard that Hailey was in a similar boat, being estranged from her family. "Hailey, when is the last time you spoke to your folks? I can help you get a message to them to let them know you're all right." Richard sounds earnest.

Hailey listens and nods. She intensely looks at Richard. "Great, but if you must know, I am *not* all right. You really are out of touch with things. I was actually looking for you when I was in the office. The other girls told me you would be there. I feel like I should do something. The conditions here are just subhuman."

SINFUL LOVE

"I'm glad you found me. Hailey, what happened? What can I do?" Instinctively, he puts his hand on her thigh for a brief moment. Hailey is startled and looks at him. Richard's eyes get intense and sorrowful as he removes his hand.

"I'm sorry, I didn't mean to make you feel uncomfortable," he says.

Richard's genuine expression catches Hailey's eye. Hailey looks into his eyes. She sees that Richard appears to have a deep concern for her, and she sees the warmth and empathy in Richard's eyes. Richard then notices a bruise on Hailey's face and reaches to touch it. Again, she recoils.

Richard is really concerned. He wonders what he was thinking. What kind of treatment did he seriously think Hailey would get in this hellhole? He feels instantly defeated and cannot verbalize this. He sighs. He realizes Hailey is still looking him in the eyes.

She senses the change to sadness and regret in his eyes.

Wow, what an empathetic man, she thinks even though he's been out to lunch apparently for so long about what's going on with the Home Girls, seemingly caring only about the money. *To stop caring,* she thought, *must be a real prison.*

"Would you like me to walk you back upstairs now? Before I say anything else that upsets you?" Richard asks, somewhat deflated and still concerned that he has made Hailey uncomfortable. Richard begins to feel that he's failed to make Hailey feel any better, and it's affecting him. "Hailey, I'm sorry if I'm being a jerk. Maybe we should go."

Hailey says, "No, I'm OK to sit with you here. You're not a jerk. You're actually quite sweet. I just don't think you honestly realize what's going on here. The Posse Men get you high and then expect sexual favors from you. I've never been treated in such a subhuman manner. It's disgusting. That's why I came to see you, to see what you could do about it, given you're number two around here," she blurted out.

"Oh my God, Hailey, I'm so sorry. I swear I didn't really know. I thought there seemed to be a mutual interest between the Home Girls and the Posse Men. I knew some of them got aggressive from time to time, but I had no idea that they force the drugs on you like that. I don't know what to say," says Richard.

"I know you're different than those animals. But I don't know how you block it out. It's really hopeless. Can you help me? I don't want any part of this. I'm actually afraid for my life," says Hailey, looking intently at Richard as they lock eyes again.

Richard looks back into Hailey's eyes, "Maybe we can spend some time together. I would like to look after you, protect you. Maybe I can keep the Posse Men away from you if we spend time together." Richard is aware of how awkward that sounded. But he is beginning to wake up from the daze of his moral sleepwalking.

He remembers James's offer about having someone to himself and wonders if he would keep his word. He suddenly feels very protective of Hailey, just seeing her there in such pain and fear.

Hailey shoots back, "That sounds good, but how are you going to do that? How are *you* going to protect me? They have guns."

Of course, Richard does not know, so he just looks away for a moment. Then he turns back, suddenly emboldened, and says, "Hailey, I'll find a way."

Hailey nods. *Maybe this guy has some guts after all*, she thinks. But she says nothing.

Then, Richard thinks, *what are you doing? What are you saying? You sound desperate. You sound like a lovesick puppy, promising what you cannot deliver.* But he cannot get over the image of finding Danielle dead on his apartment floor and how he cannot lose someone else he's begun to have feelings for again to the drugs or the violence of the Den.

Richard, now distressed, begins to get up, sensing yet another awkward moment, but Hailey startles him by grabbing his hand.

"That's really sweet, Richard. Your offer to look after me. You seem like a really good guy who's really fighting himself. Let me help you. And I could really use somebody like you looking out for me. I...I could use someone to talk to. I have so much to tell you. Would you listen?" she says.

Hearing Hailey saying his name out loud makes Richard feel a strong connection with her. "Hailey, you can tell me anything. I'm a good listener. I want to help. I'm...I'm really out of place here, too. I...I..." He sits back down, facing Hailey. He instinctively touches her face by the bruise, and for the first time, Hailey allows him to touch her. "Who did this to you?"

Hailey cries softly. "Richard, don't. You can't do anything about it, I know. These men, they...they're animals, some of them. They make you do horrible things at gunpoint."

Just then, two Posse Men approach them and say, "Enough time down here. Get back upstairs now."

Richard looks up at them with his own steely gaze.

"C'mon, man. We gave you more time than we are allowed to. Don't get us in trouble," says one of the Posse Men.

Richard nods and starts to rise, high-fives one of the Posse Men gently as if to say thank you.

Richard turns to Hailey, "Hailey, would you like to go somewhere private and spend some time together? I have my own apartment here. I have some wine. Would you like to have a glass with me? We can maybe relax together if you'd like. You can tell me what's on your mind."

Hailey looks deeply into Richard's eyes and sees that he seems authentic and genuine. She is beginning to trust him.

Hailey agrees to go. While she has some reservations, she has a feeling that she will be safe with Richard. The idea of any time spent away from the Posse Men is attractive to her. She is also starting to realize Richard may be ready to listen to her about changing his ways at the Den.

They ride up the elevator up to the fifteenth floor in silence, get out, Richard nods to the Posse Man sentry standing guard, and they both head for Richard's apartment at the rear of the floor.

They arrive at the apartment, 15W. Richard finds the front door key in his front pants pocket and reaches for the lock and unlocks both locks and opens the door. Hailey hesitates for just a moment.

"It's OK. If you want, I'll go in first." Hailey nods, and Richard goes in. She follows. Richard escorts her to an old couch in the living room. He turns on the radio to an FM station playing smooth jazz, and the band Weather Report is playing. They sit down next to one another at opposite sides of the couch.

They share a bottle of wine and Hailey, clearly still uncomfortable, eventually, says, almost out of duty, "So, do you want to have sex? Isn't that why you asked me here?" Hailey is almost surprised at the words that came out of her mouth, but she had to know if this was genuine or just another Den tryst attempt. She needs to find out if she can really trust Richard.

Richard is at first surprised at the question. But then realizes it has been several days since he is seen Hailey and maybe she has forgotten their earlier conversation about his offer to protect her in the haze of drug use. Of course, the thought of having sex with Hailey immediately races through his mind and makes his body stir. Hailey is gorgeous, and Richard is a male. But Richard's heart took over.

Richard looks Hailey in the eyes. He pauses for a moment, "Hailey, that's not why I asked you here. I'm just trying to get to know you. Please tell me what's on your mind. I'm a good listener, I want to help you. You don't have to ever feel like that with me, that you're in any way obligated to me."

Hailey is surprised by Richard's reply. Even though, she senses Richard is again being decent and respectful, she still says in an almost annoyed manner that surprises even her, "You're not gay, are you?"

Richard laughs, "No, I'm not gay, but I want you to feel comfortable around me, Hailey. You're very beautiful, smart and incredibly desirable. Any man would want to make love to you. So, do I. But it would mean everything to me if you wanted it, too. I'm just trying to get to know you first."

Hailey looks at Richard and realizes he *is* a man of far different character than the others in the Den. She also thinks, *Good answer*.

Richard is actually trying to establish a normal relationship with her in this dysfunctional world. This surprises her.

"Yeah, we can get to know each other. What's your angle?" Hailey says playfully, shielding her fun in a scowl.

Richard senses Hailey's skepticism and says, "Hailey, I just want you to be comfortable. I have no agenda, no angle. I know it would be easy to think I have one. You don't think much of me, I know because I'm here and helping this guy. I…I…I don't know. After I came here, I started to turn a blind eye to things that were important to me. After the market crash when I lost it all, something changed. It really hurt to fail. I remember my mentor Bob Lehman at Salomon Brothers always telling me I was different, I really cared about my clients, put them first. He used to say never make an investment for a client you wouldn't do with your own money, and I believed in that. Oh, man. The world is topsy-turvy right now. The economy is a mess, inflation, drugs, political stuff. Sorry, I'm just yapping away. Are you really OK? It matters to me." Richard turns toward Hailey, looking at her intensely. He moves closer to her and she does not flinch.

She wonders, what *is he doing here? The way he talks and what he's saying to me, he sounds like he actually cares how I feel*. Still, she keeps her guard up a bit.

Still not making more than partial eye contact, she replies, "Yeah, whatever." Out of the corner of her eye, she sees Richard look down and away in disappointment. *Is this guy really this genuine* she asks herself?

Suddenly, Hailey takes Richard's hand. She is about to take a chance with him. "Richard, I'm sorry. I didn't mean to behave that way. You seem like such a decent guy. I do feel a lot safer around you. I feel like maybe I can trust you, that you really do care. I think you have just lost your way in here. I can help you with that. Can we just lie down next to each other and rest for a while? I'd really like to just rest. I'm so tired."

For a moment, Hailey cannot believe she's uttered those words. But it has been so long since she has had a moment with someone she cares about, any form of human contact, a hug, an embrace, or even just simply being with them. She is also terribly lonely.

Richard smiles at Hailey and reaches to stroke her hair, moving closer to her, surprised that she allows it. "Sure. OK. Let's go to the bedroom. We can just lie next to each other on the bed if you'd like."

Richard walks slowly with Hailey, careful not to make any fast or abrupt moves that could upset her. Hailey then takes his hand in hers, and their eyes meet as they enter the bedroom silently. Richard smiles. The queen-sized bed is neatly made, which struck Hailey as odd, as she would not figure any man a neat freak at the Den. He waits for Hailey to lie down first on the left side of the bed.

Richard lies down next to Hailey, and they both turn toward one other, still fully clothed.

Richard strokes Hailey's hair. "Hailey, why don't you tell me about yourself?" They lock eyes again.

Hailey eyes sparkle as if they were plugged into an electrical outlet. She thinks this is the first time she has interacted with someone this closely and in this manner in as long as she can remember, and it feels good.

"I grew up outside Atlanta. My mom is an attorney at a big Atlanta law firm. She just made junior partner. My dad is a Baptist minister at our hometown church and has been there for thirty-five years. I love the South. I went to Temple undergrad because I wanted to go to school up north. Also, one of my best friends was going there, Wanda Williams. She graduated a year ahead of me."

"You became a Philly girl...cheesesteaks and all that?"

"I didn't eat that many cheesesteaks. I was on the track team, all four years, so that wasn't part of my diet. Still isn't."

"Wow, a track star? What was your event?"

"Relays, five thousand and ten thousand meters. I was a pretty good runner. Not Olympic caliber, but competitive. Won a few races at our heats. We won the Penn Relays in my junior year." For the first time in ages, Hailey's face brightened with pride.

"Hailey, being in good shape is probably a blessing. Your body can

SINFUL LOVE

recover faster. What…er…little body that is. I guess you won all those races in spite of your height and weight. You must generate tremendous lower body torque and foot speed I gather."

Hailey looks at Richard quizzically as he is exactly right. At five foot two and maybe ninety-five-pounds, Hailey appeared to be very petite for a runner. But Richard figures her optimal running weight was probably ten or fifteen pounds more and that she likely lost weight because of the crack use which eliminates your appetite.

"My little body does just fine. I bet I bench press more than you do!" Richard laughed. He knows she is probably correct.

"What's your story? How did you end up with this loser James Simpson?"

"We met when I was in undergrad school at Columbia. We both worked at a messenger service, just a part time job we both took for pocket change. I used to take him to this bar downtown where everyone from Wall Street used to go, Jeremy's Ale House. Had hundreds of women's brassieres hanging from the ceiling. They would serve these thirty-two-ounce quart cups of beers. We used to call them buckets. James was so out of place, he used to come in sweats with everyone else, including me dressed in suits, even the women!

"James and I used to pick up black women together at bars in Harlem. Well, he really did the intros. I was a good closer. We really had fun those days when I was still in school. James is a character. He has a great sense of humor, actually looked after me a little, I guess. James and I were always talking about going into business together. He really introduced me to some fine uptown women."

"You mean black women? So now I get it. Well, once you've had a sistah, there's no turning back!" says Hailey. Richard blushes, and Hailey laughs.

"So, tell me, what was your best pickup line that worked on us black women?" Hailey grins and leans into Richard.

Richard tries to compose himself. "Well, you know guys never tell our secrets. I don't think I own a pickup line. It didn't matter anyway. They were mostly one-night stands. Not by my choice, by the way.

Except for one woman, Michelle Brandy who I met with James at this wonderful Harlem bar. She was really cool. We dated for a while until she moved away."

"Not by your choice? Oh, you're a romantic then? You expect me to believe that with your good looks and those beautiful blue eyes that the best you could do was one-night stands, schoolboy? What was the deal with Michelle, then?"

"Hey, I got a full scholarship to Columbia. Went to NYU for graduate school in finance on a partial scholarship, too. I had no time to put a rap together. But I do have the best tunes around. I love Motown, Philly soul. I grew up on 1970s music. It was usually Al Green though that closed the deal when I'd put him on my stereo at home. Pretty boring, I guess. Michelle loved it."

"You can't go wrong with Al Green to close the deal," said Hailey, joking.

"Yup, 'I'm Still in Love with You', I mean the song," Richard said sheepishly.

"What about *your* parents?" she asked, turning a little more serious.

"My dad was a professor in the sociology department at Columbia before he retired about three years ago. He mostly writes articles for publications now on sociology or anthropology. My mom is a real estate broker. She's still very active, does well. They live upstate. They moved out of the city when Dad retired. My sister and my goddaughters live in Queens, though," says Richard. "My sister is a retired officer of the Navy. She now works for the city. The Water Department." Richard pauses for a second. *This feels so easy and natural and really good*, he thinks.

"Tell me one fun thing about you, Mr. Graf?" Hailey playfully pokes Richard in the chest. He gently grabs her hand and pulls it toward him. His heart is racing. Hailey places her hand and his on his heart and feels his rapid heartbeat. Her eyes soften, and her gaze brightens.

"Well, my grandfather came to New York City in December 1923, through Ellis Island from Bavaria, Germany, a town called Ulm. I have a copy of the manifest with his name on it. The manifest also shows who he was going to be staying with locally because back in those days if you were an immigrant, you needed both a trade or profession and a local sponsor, someone who could put you up. That was my grandfather's aunt. Now here's the interesting part. My grandfather's aunt had an apartment on the same block as my first apartment in Manhattan, which I still have, literally the next building over. And I live in the same apartment number he did! Talk about fate!"

Hailey smiles, "Wow, that's a great story!"

"It's a great New York City story, or should I say a pretty unremarkable New York story, actually, only one of many," says Richard.

"My great-great-grandparents on my father's side were slaves for a wealthy landowner in Virginia," started Hailey. "When they got their freedom, they settled in Atlanta, opened a restaurant. Not sure how, but my grandfather became a minister, so my father followed in his footsteps. My mom and I chose the law to make sure nobody we knew was ever subjected to injustice without a fight and a watchguard. There is simply too much injustice going on for black people." Richard nods in agreement.

Richard is transfixed by Hailey's story and the almost matter-of-fact way she describes her great-grandparents. "Wow, that's extraordinary," he can barely muster. "You're right. There is way too much prejudice and injustice going on. My parents taught me to be color blind, respect everyone as equals and treat people how they want to be treated, not how you want to be treated yourself."

Hailey looks intently at Richard, and she sees the authenticity in his eyes, which are slightly moist. She is beginning to fall for Richard. "Yeah, that's right," she says.

"How about a fun fact about you, Hailey?" Richard fumbles as he smiles weakly, trying to change the subject.

"Oh, I don't know. I was captain of my school debate team? So, don't mess with me. You won't win any arguments."

Richard laughs.

"You talk about boring, I'm literally the preacher's daughter. You can imagine I did not have a wild upbringing. Mostly the books, grades. I had no time for guys. I still don't. You know what I mean?" teased Hailey.

"Well, I hope present company excluded," says Richard. He notices Hailey is fading quickly, her eyes fluttering.

"Hey you're looking tired. Why don't you go to sleep," says Richard.

Hailey nods and sighs. "I would love that. I could sleep for days," says Hailey.

Richard rises from the bed on his side and peels down the sheets and comforter for her. Hailey climbs in under the covers, and Richard tucks her in.

"Good night. I'll sleep on the couch. Give a holler if you need anything. Do you want some water?" he asks.

"Yes, thank you, Richard. For everything. It will feel good to get a good night's rest for once," says Hailey. She grabs Richard's hand. "Richard..." She falls asleep immediately, her hand falling to the bed. Richard smiles and walks toward the living room, closing the bedroom door behind him. It feels odd for him to have someone else sleeping in his bed. In a flash, he remembers sleeping with Danielle, but he lets it pass. He must have truly moved on, thanks to Hailey.

The next morning, Hailey rises early, dresses, and opens the bedroom door quietly. Richard stirs and wakes from the living room couch. He gets up quickly and follows Hailey outside of the bedroom toward the front door. Hailey hesitates as she hears Richard coming toward her.

Richard rushes over to Hailey by the door, kisses her on the cheek, and she kisses him back, and he says, "I want to see you again. How about tonight? We can meet in the cafeteria in apartment 15C for dinner together, and then you can come over and stay with me."

Hailey says, "OK, I'd like that."

Richard says, "I'll meet you in the cafeteria at 6:30 PM tonight?"

SINFUL LOVE

"OK." Hailey looks up at the much taller Richard and motions him to bend down. She kisses him on the cheek.

Richard grabs the doorknob to open the door for Hailey but pauses and says, "Are you sure you want to leave?"

"No, but I need to get some things," she says.

He kisses her again on the cheek. She smiles, puts her palm on his heart, gently pushes the door open and then walks out the door. Richard is on cloud nine. He feels alive again, thinking, *Wow, she is amazing.* He reruns parts of their conversation from the night before, and it makes him swell inside.

He then turns his attention to the workday ahead, realizing he has not given work a thought since yesterday, and he has a full day's work ahead. A reality check. He quickly snaps back to work mode. Time to hit the international stock market indexes to see what the plays for the day are. As he scans his websites online, his mind is sharp, focused and laser alert for trends, market reactions, key milestones, whatever will affect the markets a particular stock, index. He is a man on a financial mission.

The day goes quickly, and Richard taps on the door to Simpson's office after 5:30PM to relay the good news.

"James, the accounts are up twenty-one percent in the past three months. I correctly shorted oil stocks and took advantage of the big play on healthcare stocks in the prostate cancer section with the release of that new wonder drug Pantitone."

The Den's investments are doing exceedingly well because of Richard's expert skill at buying and selling stocks per the predictive analysis he learned at Salomon Brothers and his trades are on fire.

Simpson is both impressed and pleased. They share a high five, and Simpson says, "Sit. Let's have a cigar to celebrate. You have exceeded even my expectations. I knew I made the right move with you."

Richard nods, and they share a smoke. Richard cannot wait now for his dinner plans with Hailey. Simpson notices Richard's excitedness.

"What's up, bro? You look all excited and shit?" Simpson says.

"I'm having dinner with Hailey tonight."

"Cool. You tap into that yet?" Simpson shot back.

"No, James. I slept on the couch, man. I'm a respectable guy!"

Simpson laughs, "Shit…Well, don't be late. And don't be too respectable next time!"

SPOILED DINNER PLANS

The Den has a makeshift cafeteria in Apartment C, which has a large, converted kitchen, where food is served buffet style and everyone in the Den on the fifteenth floor eats, unless takeout is ordered. Eaters sit in a modified living room outside the kitchen, outfitted with round tables and chairs with a TV mounted on the wall. Food is provided gratis to Den employees and residents.

After finishing up his work, Richard arrives at the cafeteria at 6:30 PM. He looks for Hailey but does not see her. He serves himself some offerings from the buffet table setup and goes to sit alone at one of the tables. One of Posse lieutenants, Roger, who has befriended Richard, sees him, and sits down with him. Roger is one of the more well-spoken Posse Men and is a decent individual overall, not typical for Posse Men. Roger knew James from the 'hood, and Roger also had a job that was a casualty of Black Monday, working at UBS as an engineering research analyst.

"Hey, did you see the new girls that came in a couple of days ago? Some real lookers. Especially that short athletic looking one. Long hair, real pretty. Smart, too. Educated. Just your type, Richard," says Roger.

Richard says, "Yes, I know, Roger. I spent the night with her. Her name's Hailey."

"Uh-oh, you're in trouble my friend, it looks like HoJo's got his sights on her, too. You better move fast. I mean watch your step."

Richard says, "Fuck HoJo. Do me a favor and tell HoJo to lay off. Hailey's...er...special and we sort of hit it off. She shouldn't have to be subjected to the likes of HoJo. He treats the girls like pieces of meat."

"Wow, I've never seen you show any interest in the girls after, Danielle. Uh...why this one?"

"Roger, she's really different. We really connected. We talked for hours. We looked into each other's eyes for the longest time. I felt like she was inside me. Plus, she comes from good stock, I can tell. Great parents. She's really intelligent. She's funny. I've got a good feeling about her, maybe us. I sure as hell know she doesn't belong here."

Roger replies, "And you can tell that all with one night? Boy, you really are a romantic. I could always tell that about you. It must have been some night. Smart, huh? Sounds like you have business and a personal interest in this woman!"

Richard laughs, "Yeah, and this is a great place to find romance or your perfect life mate. She was supposed to meet me for dinner, though. Looks like I got stood up."

"Nature of the beast, my friend. These girls all go for where the party is. You know that. That's why you can never get too attached to any of them. Plus, they steal anything that isn't nailed down. You remember that with Danielle."

"I hear you. But Hailey is different. I know I don't have to worry about that with her. Actually, I'm a little worried, I hope she didn't run into HoJo. Maybe I should go look for her," Richard replies.

"Richard, you want to hold off on that. Let it take its course. Anyway, I'm glad you're showing some interest in someone. Maybe you're ready to move on after Danielle."

Richard pauses for second "Yeah, I know, but I should have done something, Roger, to save Danielle."

SINFUL LOVE

Roger says, "You know, like James says, you couldn't do nothing. Like he says, the bitch chose the pipe and paid the ultimate price."

"Yeah, I remember. That's really crude, Roger. James wasn't really empathetic about what happened. He didn't used to be that way, treat women like they are expendable." The memory pains Richard.

Roger gets up and says good night. "Richard, you know James is in a position where he can't afford to get close to anyone. You've managed to get past that with him 'cause you guys go way back. He didn't mean anything. Let it go," he says as he walks away. Richard nods and gestures towards his friend.

In his mind, Richard had a nice plan to go for a walk with Hailey, come back to his place, play a movie on the VCR, have a bottle of wine, and then spend the night together.

He laughs to himself, saying under his breath, "What a fool I am for being such a romantic." He walks back to his apartment. He opens a bottle of wine and turns on the VCR to watch a movie, the film noir *Blade Runner*, alone.

Shortly after 8:00 PM, Richard hears a knock on his door. It is Hailey. She appears a bit ragged. Her blouse is ripped, and she smells of alcohol with a new shiner by her right eye. She asks, "Can I come in?"

Richard looks at Hailey, is immediately concerned, and opens the door as Hailey strides in. Hailey hugs Richard but looks away from him. Richard holds on to Hailey until she lets go.

"You have a really nice place. I forgot to mention it last night," says Hailey. She still does not make eye contact with Richard.

Richard nods, "Thanks. Missed you at dinner tonight. Hailey, what happened?" Richard walks toward her and sees the shiner by her eye more clearly.

"Oh, my God, what happened to your eye? Who did this to you?" Richard gently touches Hailey's face. Hailey takes Richard's hand in hers and lowers it to her waist.

Hailey explains, "I got caught up with some of the other girls and ended up being forced to go to one of the Posse Men's rooms to party.

I'm sorry, I guess I lost track of time and I couldn't get away. Like I really had a choice. They told me to say I banged my head on a railing. Really. I refused to have sex with one of them, and this is what happened!" Hailey is no longer hiding how upset she is, still not making eye contact with Richard.

Richard says softly, "You didn't bang your head on a railing. Who did this to you? HoJo? Why would he do this?"

Hailey turns, looks at Richard, and visibly upset, "Richard, what do you think we're supposed to do around here? The girls, we're...we're just fodder for these animals, don't you get it? Oh, Richard, I screwed up. What was I thinking coming to this nightmare? It's awful. Can I just use your bathroom to take a shower? I just want to wash it all away."

She looks into Richard's eyes for approval and moves toward him to put her arms around him and she hugs him for a long moment as Richard lowers his head and bear hugs her. "You can join me if you like," she says almost under her breath, near Richard's ear, not knowing if he heard. He did. Richard tingled all over.

Richard softens and strokes Hailey's head with his two hands, kisses her on the head gently, then once again wraps his arms around her, "Sure. Everything's OK now. You're safe with me. Let's wash away the bad stuff. And then let me look at that eye."

"*Let's* wash it away. You're going to help?" asks Hailey, sarcastically.

"Is that OK? I thought I heard you say you wanted some company. I'm good shower company," says Richard with a twinkle in his eye.

"Oh really? What makes you such good shower company?" laughs Hailey, for the first time in a long time. She looks at Richard as if to thank him for getting her to laugh.

"Oh, I handle a mean sponge. I can reach places no ordinary man can!" he says.

They hold hands and go to the bathroom. Under the warm shower head, they stand motionless, facing each other for the longest time. Hailey moves closer to Richard and rests her head on his chest.

SINFUL LOVE

He puts his arms around her, grabs the soap and a sponge, and washes her back. He lovingly, gently sponges off her entire body, all the while making eye contact with Hailey. She smiles and her eyes sparkle as he starts to use his open palm to smear the soap around, gently touching her breasts and the rest of her tiny fit body, bending down and on all fours to soap up her legs and feet. Hailey then spins around to wash the soap off with the shower head.

"Thank you, shower company. You sure are good company!" says Hailey. Richard smiles.

Without saying a word, they step out of the shower, Richard turns the water off and grabs a couple of towels, wrapping one around Hailey and then himself.

"You're spending the night with me," says Richard. Hailey turns to Richard and nods.

They leave the bathroom, and Hailey notices the living room couch and lies down. Remembering how quickly Hailey fell asleep the last time, Richard runs into the bedroom to grab a pillow, a sheet, and a blanket. By the time he returns to Hailey, she is already fast asleep.

He gently puts the pillow under her head, pulls the sheet over her, removes the towel and covers her with the blanket, and turns off all the lights. He hesitates, looking down at Hailey, and smiles. Her beautiful body, her smile and the sparkle in her eyes burned in his brain, and he is elated. He knows he is falling in love. He stands over here for the longest, time then makes his way to the bedroom. He reads for a bit before falling asleep himself.

Richard dreams that he and Hailey are walking outside in a field together, hand in hand. Richard wakes up and checks the alarm clock. It is 7:30 AM. He gets up and makes his way to the living room where Hailey is still sleeping. Richard goes into the kitchen to make some breakfast, eggs and toast with some cereal.

Hailey awakens to the smells. She rises and meets Richard in the kitchen. She comes up behind Richard and puts her arms around him.

Richard turns around to face her. "Hailey, honey, what happened yesterday?"

Hailey replies, "I messed up. I had some crack. It was forced on me by one of the Posse Men, LeRoy. I'm just trying to fit in here and stay under the radar. They beat on you if you don't do at least a hit or two of the drug. I thought I could manage just a hit or two, but it got away from me. Then HoJo started to hit on me. I pushed him away, and he slapped me. He tried to force himself on me, and finally one of the other guys came over and told him if she doesn't want it, HoJo, don't force her. He was furious. He actually took a swing at one of the other Posse Men. I don't remember the last hour except when I was able to gather myself and run the hell out of there. Everyone else was just like out of it. That's how I was able to get away."

Richard says, "Why did you go there if all that happens is, they get you high and then try to get you to have sex with them for more drugs and they treat you like crap? They're animals."

Hailey, embarrassed, looks away. "Yeah, but where else am I going to go? Richard, you still don't get it. It's not like we have a choice. If we don't go, they can drag us of our apartments like we are dogs. Our doors don't even lock. These guys just come and go as they please. They pull you out of your room, expect you to get high, and then have sex with them. I couldn't say no, Richard. I'm also hooked on that stuff. I had to sneak away from the party just to see you. I hope they didn't see me run out."

Richard is upset. "Hailey, that's awful. But you have to stop doing that stuff. It's a killer. Let me help you. I can get you clean." Richard puts his arm around her and helps her to the bathroom to take a shower. He touches her face gently with his hand. Hailey looks back. He thinks about how he is going to get Hailey clean in this environment, let alone away from the Posse Men.

A few minutes later. Hailey showers then dresses as Richard lies in bed. Richard notices. "Are you off now?"

"I have to get back to my room now, Richard, you know?"

"Why? Just stay here with me. It's Saturday."

Hailey is, upset. "What else am I supposed to do here? I'm sorry I can't spend as much time with you. The Posse Men will come looking for me. They already know I'm seeing you. They warned me against spending time with you. Threatened me. They don't like the competition. Don't you get it? They start mocking me. 'Where you been, ho?' they say. That's when they get physical. Especially HoJo, that pig. I'm afraid he'll do something to me and you."

Richard's expression immediately changes. He gets upset and says something he regrets, "Do something to me? I can take care of myself. You make it sound like you would almost rather be with those jerks than me. They threatened you?"

Hailey is clearly shaken by Richard's retort. "No, Richard. I'm saying I don't have a choice. This is what they expect from us. If you don't do what they say, it can get ugly. It's about time you get that." Hailey turns and leaves running out of the bedroom and the apartment, leaving the door open.

"Wait," Richard calls out after her, immediately feeling guilty and wanting to take back his remark. He gets up from the bed to go after Hailey, swings open the door, but it is too late. She has gone into the hallway. Richard slams the door and grabs his head in his hands.

He has to do something, get Hailey off this path that may kill her. He has to take a stand. In frustration, he claps his two hands against the side of his head.

"You idiot," he mumbles to himself. He realizes he has to get ready for work and trudges to the bedroom to clean up and make the bed and choose his clothes after he showers. He knows he needs to do something. It is driving him crazy. It kills him that he cannot be with Hailey. He can't get the image out of his mind of her running off, and he can't do anything about it. Or can he?

LEFTOVERS

About an hour after Hailey leaves, Richard goes to breakfast in the cafeteria. He sees Hailey there with several other Home Girls at one of the round tables with several of the Posse Men. Richard has a seat at an adjacent table and looks toward Hailey, who turns her head away, avoiding his gaze. Richard still feels terrible from what he said to her that morning and rises from his table to approach her, but then Hailey and the Posse Men get up and leave together. The other girls fidget and dance about. The men are raucous and loud.

HoJo sneers at Richard to stay away. Richard stops in his tracks. He knows he has to get to work with a busy day ahead, and this is a distraction. He gathers himself and heads to his office. He feels sick about Hailey going off with the other Home Girls and Posse Men. But he must concentrate on his work, knowing any lapse in concentration can cost big dollars.

Richard does not see Hailey for the next two days. He is miserable, and it shows. His imagination is running wild, thinking about Hailey having to serve the Posse Men and what they must be doing to her. It is killing him. He is visibly affected at work and takes the afternoon off, feigning sickness. He is tempted to look for Hailey but remembers Roger's warning not to.

SINFUL LOVE

He runs into Roger outside his office in Apartment A as he is leaving for his sick time. "Roger, I haven't seen Hailey in two days. Have you seen her?" Richard looks desperate.

"Hey, pull yourself together, man. I know you really dig her. But she's part of the stable, man. You need to accept that. That means you get leftovers."

"Leftovers? Fuck that, I can't accept that, Roger. I need to get her out of there, away from that scene. I really care about her. I mean, how do you condone what the rest of your guys do to those girls?"

"Hey, it's not me, man. They're not my guys. I'm not in charge of them. And I don't partake. It's only a handful of them that do that shit, treating the girls bad. I don't disrespect women, most of the posse men don't, either," says Roger.

"They why do you tolerate it, Roger? You don't come from that!"

"Whoa, you better dial it back a few notches, bro. The girls take the edge off the guys, man. Look, these girls come here looking for a party and the drugs, and they expect the sex stuff. They willingly give it up for the drugs, man. I know your girl is probably not that way, but she's here, she's part of it, so she has to pay her dues, man."

Richard is flustered. "This is fucked up, Roger. I'm going to go down there and find her and pull her out of there. I don't care." He gets up from his desk, but Roger stops him, chest to chest.

Roger says, in a measured tone, "You can't go down there. I'll see if I can free her up from the rest of the pack for a while. I'll bring her to you. It's too dangerous for you to try to intercede. Even though you help most of those guys out with investments, you will be crossing a line with them. You have to understand that." Richard backs down.

"If you could do that, I'd owe you one, man," he says.

"Richard, you know we're not supposed to become attached to these girls. You remember what happened to you with Danielle. It's too bad you didn't meet Hailey under different circumstances. You're a good guy. She seems like a great gal. I'm sorry about this. But it is what it is."

"Roger, I can't undo what is done. I really like her. I have to protect her. What kind of man am I if I don't? And I am not going to let happen to her what happened to Danielle. No way."

Roger puts his hands-on Richard's shoulders. "I'll do what I can, bro."

Richard thanks his friend but says, "Roger, I just can't sit back and do nothing."

Roger remarks, "Geez, what are you in love with her or something?"

Richard nods ."Yeah, I think so."

"All right. I'll see what I can do. Geez, man. Falling in love…"

Richard replies, "Thanks, bud."

As he is walking away, Roger says, "You should talk to James about this. Didn't you tell me he said he might make an exception for you if you found someone you liked? Maybe you could keep her in your room. Get her cleaned up. You should look into that. Catch James at the right moment, you never know."

Richard nods and acknowledges Roger. He hits himself on the forehead. Of course. He remembers James alluded to that. How could he forget. It is now time to play that card. But he objects to the sound of Roger's "keep her in your room" like Hailey's a possession.

No, I would protect her in my room. Take care of her. Nurse her back to health, he thinks. Richard is emboldened and goes off to have that conversation with James.

SOME GOOD ADVICE

Hailey is chatting with Gloria, one of the other Home Girls, in between partying in the apartment they share. They are talking about Hailey's shiner from the previous party session.

"That bastard HoJo hit me again because I wouldn't have sex with him. If it wasn't for Nicole, he could have really hurt me. She bailed me out by agreeing to have sex with that animal."

Gloria, an attractive tall black woman with short hair in her mid-twenties, says, "Damn, girl, you found yourself a nice white guy. He's like the number two man around here. You would be smart to hold onto that, honey, play that ace card. He's your meal ticket."

Hailey replies, "I really like him. He's really good to me."

"Girl, you will not find anything close to that around here. You better close that deal."

"Yeah, but how do I do that?"

Gloria, says, "Girl, get number two to go to number one to ask him to protect your ass. But be careful with your white guy. He had a girlfriend before. Her name was Danielle. Boy, he was into her. He couldn't get enough of that sugar. She looked *real* good. But she got hooked on the pipe, and it did her in. Dropped dead right on the floor in his crib. He found her just lying there. Eyes wide open.

Wrecked your boy. Didn't know if he would ever get over it. But I guess he did if he's taken a fall for you. He's a good guy. Nobody has anything bad to say about him. He's bought us dinner a couple of times."

Hailey nods and processes everything. "Gloria, we have to do something about the violence around here. These guys go too far."

"Girl, you and I are the only two women here coherent enough to even have this conversation! The rest of them are just like freakin' zombies! They probably don't even notice it when they're getting beat on, or worse, raped," says Gloria.

Hailey exhales. "Gloria, I got to go see him, Richard. I was so mad at him that I avoided him for two days. But that was really mean. I know he didn't mean anything when he said to me, that I'd rather be with these animals. I know he didn't mean it. He was just frustrated, too."

"Girl run to him. He needs you. Sounds like he could be hurting."

Hailey says, "I know I was just thinking that. Let me sneak over there. If you run into the Posse boys, just tell them I went to the kitchen or something."

"Ha, girl, you crazy! Ain't nobody eatin' around here!" Hailey leaves their apartment, carefully looking in all directions as she closes the door. She can't remember the last time she enjoyed food.

Richard finishes his work, has dinner delivered from his favorite takeout chicken place, which he picks up from the lobby, and takes it to his room. He starts to serve his dinner and then hears a knock at the door. His heart stops.

"Hailey?" Richard runs to the door, sees Hailey standing there, a bit disheveled, with a small red mark on her cheek, but Richard does not care. He wraps his arms around her lifts her up into the apartment and closes the door. "Hailey, I'm so sorry. I'm such a jerk. Please forgive me. I have no right to judge anybody. Come here. Don't ever leave like that again."

Hailey smiles at Richard and places her hand on his cheek. Richard almost loses it. He then takes her head in his hands and kisses her on both cheeks, stroking her cheeks. He notices the red mark. "Hailey, what happened?"

"It got a little rough."

Richard says, "Come with me. Let's get you cleaned up." He picks her up and carries her to the bathroom.

"Richard, put me down!" says Hailey, laughing. Richard gently lowers her, and Hailey walks into the bathroom.

Richard enters the bathroom and begins to undress her, and Hailey starts to undress Richard. They start kissing. Richard turns on the shower. They step in together.

"Will you be my shower buddy again?" says Hailey looking mischievously at Richard.

Richard is aroused. Hailey grabs the soap and the sponge and starts lathering up Richard from head to toe, taking her time, making sure to get in every crack and crevice. She notices Richard's fit body. She stops at a huge scar he has on the right size of his waistline. She looks up at him with a serious expression.

"Oh, it's from a burst appendix. Happened during the summer before my senior year in college. Was pretty touch and go. Doctor says I could have died, but it had walled itself off or something, so the poison didn't get into my bloodstream. Lost a good part of my lower bowel, though. My German constitution, it saved my life. I'm indestructible. Can't you tell?"

Hailey stands up, hands Richard the soap and the sponge, and turns her back to Richard, and says, "Would you get my back, my dear?"

Richard smiles and slowly soaps up Hailey's body again, starting with her back, then her front, bending down on all fours to soap up Hailey's legs and feet, all the while making eye contact. He then stands and removes the detachable shower head from its holder. He uses the shower head to wash the soap off Hailey's body, making his way down her back then her front and then toward her privates. He bends down as if to kiss her there, but Hailey gently takes his head in her hands and brings it up to her. She kisses him as if to say, "not tonight."

Richard is disappointed for just a moment, but he grabs towels for them both, and they dry off. They walk to the bedroom together, still in their towels, and Hailey grabs Richard's hand as if to say everything is OK. Richard dresses in silence in the bedroom. Hailey, still in the towel, left her clothes in the bathroom.

Hailey breaks the ice. "Hm, that was nice. I'm a little hungry. You? Got some food?"

"Yeah, I ordered takeout from my favorite chicken place for us. Never got to eat it. Somehow I got distracted."

"Oh, I don't know. You seemed pretty intent on what you were doing. Worked up an appetite, did you?"

"Hailey, you really want me to answer that?"

"You don't have to. Your little man told me," she laughed.

Richard laughed, thinking the courting and foreplay was fun. Her reference to his arousal was especially fun, although he was disappointed it never went any further. This time.

They share Richard's takeout food at the small circular table in the kitchen, still wrapped only in towels.

Hailey says, "Hey, that was good. May I have some more?"

Richard says, "Sure." He proceeds to serve up some more of the chicken with broccoli and rice and a side of fried green plantains, called tostones. Gold old fashioned uptown Manhattan chicken takeout.

"Hailey, no matter what happens, I want you to stay with me until I can figure this out." Richard pauses to think. "Don't leave this room. I will take care of you. I don't want you to spend another day out there with those animals. I'll figure out how to keep you safe. I'll talk to James. I've got to put a stop to this drugging and sex ring going on here. It's deplorable. Hailey, do you *want* to stay with me?" Richard feels like he is babbling, speaking fast.

Hailey is touched by Richard finally taking some action. "Richard, yes, I want to be with you, only you. OK, I'll do as you say, I'll hide out and stay here. I'll keep the door locked and let no one in. God bless you." With the drugs now wearing off and the partying and cavorting

SINFUL LOVE

becoming a bad memory, she says, "I just can't think or act straight while I'm on the drugs. I need to get off it. I need to pull it together. Richard, can you help me get clean?"

Richard looks Hailey dead in the eye and says, "Yes, I will. Stay with me. I'll get you clean. I'll protect you. I really care about you."

Hailey goes over to Richard, touches his cheek, and says, "Yes, Richard, I will stay with you. You always make me feel safe. I...I need to get off this drug and out of this horrible situation. I just want to get my life back. If you could help me with that, I'd be so grateful to you."

Richard bends down and hugs Hailey. "Hailey, I'll help you any way I can."

Hailey looks at Richard and buries her head in his shoulder. "I care about you, too. You're a good man. But what are you going to do about the Posse Men? They'll come looking for me."

Richard strokes Hailey's head leaning against his shoulder. He reaches down and kisses her on her forehead. "Let me worry about that," he says. "I will just go to James and demand that you stay with me and that I won't take no for an answer."

Richard has quickly fallen in love with Hailey, which surprises him, and he knows it is no infatuation, like perhaps it had been with Danielle, even though he thought he genuinely cared about her. Still the sex was amazing with Danielle. He wondered when he'd get to experience that with Hailey.

What would it be like? he thinks.

Hailey feels relieved that Richard has really stepped up for her and looks into his eyes and smiles. They sit on the couch in Richard's living room.

Hailey takes Richard's hand and asks, quietly, "Richard, tell me about Danielle?"

Richard is momentarily shaken but measures his words. "Why? Who told you? Why would you ask me about that?"

"Gloria, one of the Home Girls, my *roommate*, told me the whole story."

Richard then pauses, collects himself, and continues, "I'm sorry.

She was…she was someone I cared about. But she could not stop doing crack. It killed her. I should have done more for her. I tried everything," he says with a big sigh, then he puts his head in his hands.

"But it wasn't your fault, Richard. She made a wrong choice," says Hailey, rubbing Richard's hand.

Richard's head snaps up, and he removes his hands. "Yeah, I know, but I still feel responsible. That's why I'm not going to let the same thing happen to you. Everybody who gets close to me…"

Hailey sits next to Richard, strokes his head, and kisses him flush on the mouth for the first time. Richard is startled and kisses her back. Hailey has seen Richard at a vulnerable moment and now she is feeling protective of him. She hops on his lap and is now fully embraced with him and kissing him.

"It's OK. It's not your fault. I'm here," she wraps her arms tighter around Richard.

They embrace for a long moment, followed by another kiss. They look at each other for a long pause. Richard smiles broadly.

"Hey, let's have a glass of wine. Would you like that?" He's still savoring the moment.

Hailey says, "Of course." She smiles broadly and is the happiest she can recall being in some time. "Tell me more about you, Mr. Graf," as she looks intently in his eyes.

Richard opens a bottle of wine, motions for Hailey to sit next to him, and begins, "I was in finance, doing really well, on a fast track to be vice president at the Wall Street firm Salomon Brothers. When the stock market crash happened, I lost everything. One day, I get a call from James Simpson. He wants me to manage the finances for his new business. I say I'll think about it. I almost don't want to know what it's about.

"I guess I knew deep down it was likely something illegal. Turns out, I was right, but it was too late. I had already agreed to sign up. I told myself I was just handling the finances, maybe for a year or two to get back on my feet. I had nothing to do with the drugs part, of people getting hurt, killing themselves, selling themselves, I kept telling myself. I don't know what I was thinking. I was in denial. I know it's wrong, but now I'm stuck. I'm also making a lot of money. I've saved over three million dollars in just over two years!"

Hailey stops him short. "Richard, you're better than this. That money is blood money. You don't want any part of it. I lost my way, too. After I graduated from Temple, I started Columbia Law School. A couple months in, my roommate, Nicole and I, we started going out to parties and stuff together. Then, she introduced me to her friend Denise—you know, she also came here with me—who introduced me to crack. For a while I resisted, told them no. But eventually, I broke down. First it was once in a while. Then I didn't realize Nicole had become addicted. And then I also got hooked, and you know, you start getting desperate, doing crazy things just to get more drugs." Richard's eyes are locked on Hailey, his concern intense in his fiery but loving gaze on her.

"Wait! the Nicole who came in here with you?" Hailey nods.

"Crack makes you do things you would never do," Hailey continues. "I ended up getting high in abandoned, burned-out buildings uptown with mattresses strewn on the floors. People getting high everywhere, stumbling around like zombies. It was disgusting. I couldn't stop. And then one day, one of these Posse Men picked us up in Harlem promising drugs and food and a place to stay and brought us here. I didn't want to go, but I was with Nicole and Denise. We would hang out together with the Posse Men. They would protect me from HoJo. But I haven't seen either of them in over a month, not even with other Posse Men. In the very beginning, they split us up. They were staying in an apartment on the west wing and I was over here. Richard, have you heard anything? I haven't seen them, and nobody says anything to me."

"I don't know, Hailey. I just know there was a big fuss last week. They said a couple of the Home Girls overdosed. Oh, no! I hope it wasn't your friends. I'll find out. Nobody told you? Of course not. Geez." Richard moves toward Hailey and stands close to her. He bends down to comfort her. She puts her head on his chest.

"Oh my God, Richard, no! if it was them, I can't take it," Hailey cries softly. Richard puts his arms around her. "Oh Richard. Think about it. My father is a *pastor*, and my mother is a well-known criminal lawyer back home. I've disgraced my family."

"Hailey, you haven't disgraced anyone. You just got caught up in something in a weak moment. You were in the wrong place at the wrong time. It happens to all of us. It's happened to me. The first thing we need to do is get your clean. Then I've got to get and keep you away from the rest of the Home Girls pack and the Posse Men. It's just not safe for you. For now, you'll stay with me."

Hailey smiles at Richard. "We also need to do something to help the rest of the girls. We can't let that happen to anyone else. Richard, how on Earth did we end up here? But I'm so glad I met you. You are an honest, decent man. I really care about you."

Richard smiles and Hailey rushes to kiss him. They embrace. They walk to the bedroom to turn in for the night. After they undress, they lie on the bed and continue talking in their underwear.

"Hailey, you're right. I am better than this. I never thought I would have ever sold my soul to the devil like this. I've got to make this right somehow. Starting with the ill treatment of the tenants and the Home Girls. We started fixing up some of the tenant's apartments, but we need to really get them on our side."

"Richard, you need to be smart. Be careful. You know you can't depend on James to back you unless there's some kind of financial or other benefit to him. That's the only language a gangster like him understands, no matter how well you think you know him. You need some kind of leverage. Choose your battles carefully."

"Wow, you really got this well scoped out. And you're dead on. But I have to try. I need to try to make a difference now." Richard can't believe the words he's saying, but he feels better, more alive and more purposeful than he's felt in quite some time.

Richard rises from the bed, walks into the bathroom, retrieves Hailey's dirty clothes from the bathroom floor, and handwashes them in the bathroom sink, and then hangs them to dry. He makes a mental note to get more clean clothes for her. He returns to the bedroom, Hailey is waiting.

"I was just washing out your clothes. They should be dry by morning. I have a long T shirt you can wear over your undies if you'd like. It's in the top drawer of the dresser. Feel free to wear any of my clothes. Other than the pants of course. You would swim in them!"

Hailey looks at Richard in appreciation. "Thank you." She puts on the T-shirt from the dresser and motions to him, and then they go to bed. Soon, they're in each other's arms in a warm embrace.

Hailey looks Richard dead in the eye. "Richard, I so want to make love to you, my darling, but I'm, I'm just not ready. I'm sorry. I hope you understand."

The words jolt Richard, who is already aroused in anticipation that this may be the night.

Richard looks at Hailey for the longest as their eyes meet, "It's OK, Hailey. I want you more than I've ever wanted anyone in my life. But I can wait. When you're ready, you'll let me know. But first let's get you better."

Hailey smiles with a tear trickling down her face. For the first time in a long time, she feels safe as she melted into Richard's arms, kissing him before falling asleep in his arms.

Richard is still so aroused. He bites his lip and laughs to himself about his predicament. But the feeling in his heart carries him through his anticipation.

WHERE'S HAILEY?

Hailey has been staying in Richard's apartment secretly for several days. Richard overhears from two of the Posse Men talking as he makes his way into his office in the main apartment.

"Where is that bitch Hailey? She must have gone hiding or some shit. Haven't seen her all week."

One of the other Posse Men says, "I bet she's been hanging out with the white guy, the accountant. He's got quite a hard on for her. Ha, HoJo threatened to kill her ass if she went near the white boy again. Man's crazy as shit."

They notice Richard and bellow to him, "Hey, white boy! Where's your girl, huh? You got her stashed somewhere?"

Richard plays dumb. "I wish. I don't know where she is."

Just then, James Simpson strides into the main apartment. "Hailey, eh? Your little sweetheart, eh, Richard? I've been noticing you, too. Little birdie told me!"

Richard walks over to James Simpson, bends down, "Hey, James, can I speak to you?"

"Later, my friend. Got some business to take care of. Can this wait until I get back? If it can't, just do what you have to do, I got your back." Simpson abruptly leaves the office.

SINFUL LOVE

Richard has planned to talk to Simpson about having Hailey stay with him permanently. But all week Simpson seems preoccupied with other matters as it turns out he has acquired a rival gang's operation in Jamaica, Queens, and is setting up a new operation there. Richard hasn't been consulted on the expansion yet. Simpson has been spending much time away from the Den all week finalizing arrangements. Still, James has told him to do what he has to do, so as far as Richard is concerned, keeping Hailey in his apartment is his call and he believes James will support it.

Richard has been nursing Hailey back to health, doting on her in his apartment all week, under the radar.

On the third day, Richard sits next to Hailey on the bed. He wipes her brow with a hand towel. "How are you doing? Is your skin still creeping? How do your teeth feel? You should start to feel some things returning to normal by now. I made you some chicken soup. Was tough to find the right ingredients. I had to borrow some from the kitchen."

Hailey sits up in bed. "Yes, I feel a lot better. You're right, the itching has stopped, and I can feel my teeth again. They've stopped tingling. I'm just so tired, Richard."

"It's OK, Hailey. You can rest as long as you need. Your body has been through a shock. That stuff just sucks the life out of you. Rest is the best cure along with lots of liquids and Mr. Graf's chicken soup!"

Richard holds the bowl in front of Hailey and spoons several servings of the soup into Hailey's mouth. He kneels next to her on the bed to steady himself and is really enjoying feeding Hailey back to health.

"Hm, this is delicious. Hand me that, Richard, I don't need anyone feeding me. I'm OK," says Hailey. She looks at Richard lovingly.

Richard smiles and hands the bowl and spoon to Hailey on a small tray. He then starts to get up from the bed when Hailey grabs him turning him toward her. Richard looks back at Hailey and knows instinctively to lean down and kiss her. She rests the bowl on the tray on the end table by the bed and takes Richard's face in her hand to guide his lips to hers, pulling him on top of her. They kiss for a long moment. Richard rises and looks back at Hailey, their eyes locking as he exits the bedroom.

"I gotta go back to work. I'll be back later, love." Richard walks toward the front door and he heads out.

⁓

"HOW DO YOU FEEL TODAY?" Richard asks Hailey on the sixth morning while Hailey still rests in bed. He sits next to her and wipes her brow. The glow has returned to her face.

"I feel much better. I can feel the cravings diminishing. I feel like I can think again, thanks to you." She smiles at Richard. He smiles back. "I feel like I can get up today and be about. It's been like, five days?"

"Six. You're looking much better. Got some color back in your skin. Your eyes aren't so puffy. Black circles are gone," says Richard as he leans in close to Hailey, but it costs him a kiss, as Hailey surprises him, feigning shock.

"Got more color? Is that a joke or something?" she says.

"I mean you look healthy again. Your skin is glowing. You were a little pale. Why is it I feel like I'm digging myself in deeper the more I talk? Are you hungry? How about some bacon and eggs? I slipped Roger a twenty the other day to get us some extra special breakfast stuff when he went shopping. He dropped it off a little while ago."

"Oh, that sounds yummy. I'll meet you in the kitchen. I'm just going to take a shower first," Hailey is smiling toward Richard. He of course interprets that as an invitation.

Hailey undresses in the bathroom and opens the shower curtain and turns the hot water on. Moments later, she smiles as she hears the door open, quietly, as Richard sneaks inside the shower comes up from behind to Hailey. Hailey laughs. Richard wraps his arms around her as she snuggles up against Richard. Richard gently turns Hailey toward him. He is again both aroused and smitten looking at his beautiful, exotic, shapely, petite woman he is in love with.

Richard stands almost a foot taller than Hailey. With the water running over their bodies, Richard begins to rub soap slowly and gently on Hailey with his hands, caressing her breasts, shoulders, neck, back, and then he kneels down to place soap on her legs and between her legs, all while keeping his eyes on Hailey's to see her reaction, to make sure she is not upset. He smiles. She smiles back. His heart is racing.

He gently pulls Hailey closer to him, under the showerhead, to wash the soap off, using his hands again across her body in gentle motions to wash the soap away. He again gently takes Hailey's face in his hands and kisses her repeatedly, then moves his hands down her back to her behind.

Hailey notices, "Wow, your heart is racing. And your little friend is at attention!"

She puts her hand on his heart. They eye each other.

Richard almost convulses. "It's you, Hailey. I've never felt like this before. I love you."

Hailey smiles for a moment, realizing that Richard's expression is really genuine. She puts her arms around Richard's neck and kisses Richard on the lips while the warm water washes over them. Hailey rubs up against Richard and he almost convulses.

Richard then starts to kiss Hailey on the neck, working his way down her breasts, stomach, waist, her thighs, slowly, kissing her so gently, squatting down until he reaches her vagina, kissing her gently up and down each inner thigh as he kneels down directly in front of her. He looks in her in the eyes again, then gently spreads her legs apart and performs oral sex on her, gently and then rhythmically, cupping his hands-on Hailey's small, tight butt and applying pressure moving her toward him. Richard never takes his eyes off Hailey's.

Hailey moans as Richard increases his rhythm. She calls out Richard's name several times.

Several crescendos later, Hailey is feeling lightheaded and flushed and she stumbles and loses her balance in the shower. Richard stands up, catches Hailey and scoops her up in his arms and carries her out of the shower, turning off the water in one motion. He then snatches two towels in his right hand and carries Hailey to the bedroom nearby and toward the bed.

He places the towels down on the bed and then carefully lays Hailey on them and dries her gently as she relaxes. He then pulls the sheets up to cover Hailey. Soon it is Hailey's turn, and she pleases Richard as he twists and turns in bed in pleasure. Then Hailey climbs on top of Richard riding Richard up and down for what seems like an eternity to Richard. Richard then rolls Hailey over and then finish with Richard whispering, "I love you," over and over until they crescendo together. Hailey holds Richard so tightly, not letting him go. She strokes Richard hair and kisses him. Finally, Richard rolls over onto his side after he is no longer aroused.

They rest for hours in each other's arms.

Finally, several hours later, Richard wakes up, his stomach growling.

Richard whispers to Hailey, "Still hungry for some breakfast?"

Hailey groggily responds, "OK." Then she rolls over and puts her head on Richard's chest, which she kisses and then melts into his arms. Richard is beaming as he gently strokes her hair. He feels alive for the first time in years, maybe ever.

"You know, I was supposed to make breakfast, but I didn't. That was hours ago. Don't even know if it's still time for breakfast. What time is it?"

"Hm, yes, you were too busy dining on something else." says Hailey jokingly. "Breakfast still works. Doesn't matter what time it is. Hm, that was a good rest. You really put me to sleep, Mr. Graf!"

Richard gets up from the bed with an amused look on his face like the proverbial Cheshire cat. "I'll go get breakfast started while you get dressed. Or don't get dressed. Come any way you like to eat!" he says, looking at his watch which reads 5:30 PM. They had been asleep for six hours together!

∼

SINFUL LOVE

THE NEXT MORNING, Hailey wakes up and starts orally pleasing Richard before he is even awake. Richard wakes up, with Hailey still at it, and wordlessly, they make passionate love for well over an hour. Afterward, they sit in bed, engaging in some pillow-talk and enjoying each other.

"Do you always try to have oral sex with someone on the first date?"

Richard blushes. He is a bit flustered. "First date, no, I...I...I don't. Of course not. I just wanted to please you, and I thought you wanted me to. I'm usually much shyer than this. I don't know what came over me. I gather you enjoyed it! Besides, what about all last week when you were detoxing. Wasn't that a bunch of dates? I mean technically they were, no?"

Hailey smiles. "That doesn't count. You were doing your civic duty! Oh, I think I have a good idea what came over you. You like sistahs." She kisses Richard.

Richard smiles. "I do, yes. Especially this one."

She looks in his eyes for what seems like an eternity, and Richard is transfixed. "What do you see when you look in my eyes?" he finally asks.

"Oh, I'm not sure yet. Those blue eyes tell me a lot. They change color sometimes. I haven't figured that part out yet. I can see that maybe I can trust you. Jury's still out," Hailey says playfully.

"Maybe? Yes, you can, Hailey, trust me. I hope by now you can really see that!"

Hailey looks into Richard's eyes this time for a minute or so before rising up from the bed, grabbing her clothes, and saying, "Jury is still out. I'm going to take a shower and then off to work you go young man."

Richard nods, reluctantly.

After a full week of detox for Hailey and after Richard has gone off to work, Hailey leaves Richard's apartment to go back to her room to get the remainder of her belongings that the other Home Girls did not steal. She tries to do so stealthily but unfortunately crosses paths with HoJo.

HoJo bumps into Hailey and says, "Hey, girl, where have you been?"

"I've been sick with the flu. I was staying in the infirmary to get better," says Hailey, quickly thinking.

HoJo gave her a puzzled look as if to say, "What the fuck are you talking about?" But then straightens up his twisted face.

"Good. Well, I'm glad you're better," he bellows. "Tonight, seven o'clock, be at my room. It's party time! Be there, or else I'm not gonna be so nice, woman!"

"I will," Hailey unconvincingly hides her gaze and walks away. She breathes a sigh of relief for the moment as HoJo walks away but knows HoJo now has her on his radar.

Hailey goes back to Richard's apartment and lets herself in with the key Richard lent her. Richard comes in after 6:30 PM again with takeout food delivery, so he can hide the extra food for Hailey. Hailey does not tell Richard about her encounter with HoJo as she does not want to upset Richard. They curl up together to watch TV. Richard puts on *Seinfeld* and soon they are engrossed in the nuanced humor of the sitcom. Richard starts talking about business.

"James is opening another location in Jamaica, Queens, he acquired from a rival gang. He finally told me this morning. I was surprised that he didn't tell me sooner, but he really shields me from most of the unpleasant things about the business."

Hailey asks, "Are you going to have to go there?"

"I don't know. I hope not. I just need to know how much cash they bring in and what the cadence is. We still have to get the cash out of the country to the bank in the Caymans. James will probably send one of my accountants over there to run the finances under my watchful eye. I don't yet know how big the operation is. I guess I'll find out. Whatever it is, just lay low here until I figure it out."

"Mr. Graf watch your step. Make sure you come home to me," Hailey kisses Richard.

HOJO'S LAST STAND

That night there is a big party with the Home Girls and a number of the Posse Men in one of their apartments with HoJo holding court brandishing his gun, pointing it around at all the Home Girls bellowing to them to "Git your ho asses over here and chow down!" referring to his manhood. He is already drunk and abusive.

Other Posse Men just bust a gut laughing with their own girls sitting on their laps. In the background, rap music blasts the Beastie Boys.

As it is after 9:00 PM, HoJo looks up, pushes away his latest conquest, and yells out, now drunk and high himself, "Where's that little college girl bitch? I told her to be here. She stood me up. I'm going hurt that bitch." Drunk, he stumbles to the floor and passes out. The rest of the Posse Men and Home Girls snicker and continue to party one into the night.

THE NEXT DAY, Hailey is cleaning Richard's apartment. It is just after 4:00 PM when Hailey hears a knock at the door. Whoever it is knocks three times, the signal that would normally let her know it is Richard. She opens the door and says, "Richard, you're home early—"

But it is HoJo, steaming mad, who pushes open the door, rushes in, slaps Hailey, grabs her by the hand, and says, "Bitch, you don't stand me up! You think you can get away with this? I'm going to teach you a lesson!" HoJo slaps Hailey several more times and then forces himself on her. When he's done, he literally drags Hailey behind him by the arm toward Richard's office at the other end of the floor in Apartment A.

HoJo enters Richard's office, still pulling Hailey by the arm. Richard rises from his desk. HoJo tosses Hailey at Richard's feet. "Here's your girlfriend, punk. What's left of her."

Richard rushes to Hailey and picks her up in his arms, as other Home Girls just outside the office come in to see what the commotion is about. First, they scream and also approach Hailey and help her up to her feet. Hailey is bruised, bleeding slightly from her mouth. Richard motions to them to take Hailey to safety. He eyes HoJo knowing now this is the final showdown.

"HoJo, you've gone too far!" says one of the Home Girls.

HoJo snarls, "Bitch, come over here and do me right!"

Richard stands up and calls out, "HoJo, you're an animal! You don't get it, do you? You don't want to mess with me. Now you just crossed the line."

HoJo takes out a gun, points it at Richard, and bellows, "I could shoot you right here, you little maggot!"

Richard backs up and then calls his bluff. "You're a big man waving that gun, eh? Makes you real big. You shoot me...what's James going to do to you?"

HoJo then comes right at Richard who instinctively sidesteps him. HoJo swings at Richard, who blocks the blow and counters with a karate fist to HoJo's midsection followed by a powerful fist to HoJo's face sending the bigger man tumbling backward to the floor. As HoJo struggles to get up, Richard connects on a thundering roundhouse kick to HoJo's face sending HoJo sprawling backward to the floor landing with a huge thud, with his head bangingly solidly on the floor, but still holding on to the weapon. HoJo is out cold on the floor.

The fracas has attracted a crowd of Home Girls who are deriding HoJo, cursing him, happy to see someone finally taking him down a notch.

"Yeah, fuck you, HoJo. Take a licking now, bitch!" yells one of the girls.

Richard turns his back on HoJo and goes to check on Hailey. He bends down for a moment, then motions to one of the nearby Home Girls "Hilda, can you take Hailey to the infirmary? She really needs to be looked at. I'll meet you there."

Hilda nods, and Richard lifts Hailey up with Hilda's help. Meanwhile, HoJo, bleeding from the mouth, has gathered himself, stumbling and is making his way towards Richard.

With Richard's back turned, he sees HoJo running toward him in his periphery, and HoJo whacks Richard with a glancing blow on the back of the head with the gun butt. Richard falls face down on the floor. HoJo pounces on him and starts beating on Richard's shoulders and head. Richard tries his best to cover up his head, but he is groggy from the first blow with the gun butt. Richard rolls over and manages to get a few shots in to HoJo's head but is too dazed to do anything but cover up as HoJo wildly comes at him. He kicks up at HoJo and temporarily knocks him aside, but HoJo is relentless and right on top of Richard again, who is too groggy to stand.

Other Posse Men have arrived, some are trying to talk HoJo down, some are just standing there laughing. HoJo continues to beat on Richard who has completely covered up, protecting himself. Roger arrives too late. Roger pleads with HoJo and tries to confront him, but HoJo pushes Roger away and turns back to a fallen Richard pointing the gun right at him, cocking the gun as if he is about to shoot.

Then James Simpson strides in. In one swift motion, he pulls his pistol and shoots HoJo behind the right ear, and HoJo tumbles dead to the floor. Simpson turns to everyone and says matter-of-factly to all within earshot range, "My man Richard is untouchable. You got that?

And from now on his girl Hailey is with Richard and nobody else. And we don't beat up no girls. No more. That shit stops now. Everybody down?" He turns to look at HoJo bleeding out on the floor. "Fucking, HoJo. Why, man, why? Stupid mothafucka."

The Posse Men tacitly agree as they nod or say, "Yeah, boss," in unison.

Gerard, a Posse Man who was close to HoJo, goes over to the fallen Richard, grabs him by the arm, and says menacingly, "You best watch your back, punk!"

Richard rises unsteadily and pushes his arm away and takes a defensive stance, ready to defend himself, bleeding from his nose and mouth. But he can barely stand.

Simpson spins around, pulls his gun out again, and approaches Gerard, and puts the gun against his temple. Gerard backs off screeching in pain, as the muzzle is still hot from the bullet that was fired.

Simpson says, "There will be no retaliation against Richard or Hailey. If I find out anyone tries, it will be that mothafucka's last day on this planet, do you understand?"

Gerard cowers and nods, rubbing his head. There was a murmur, and then the rest of the Posse Men nod. Gerard says yes as well.

Simpson says, "Good. Now carry on, mothafuckas. Pass this on to all you other Posse Men, motherfuckas. Now I got shit to do. Yo, Roger, take care of the body." He then looks at Richard and says without any emotion. "Yo, get cleaned up, man."

Richard pantomimes, "Thanks."

Simpson replies, "Aw right."

As Simpson walks out, he is shaking and smiles. While he is handy with a gun, he's hardly a gangster, but he likes playing the role, remembering Brian DePalma's movie *Scarface* which he and Richard had watched it numerous times together back in the day.

∽

RICHARD SLOWLY GATHERS himself and wipes the blood away from his forehead and temple with some paper towels handed to him. He says he is all right and that he needs to check on Hailey. Richard goes to see Hailey in the ad hoc infirmary, where she is recovering on one of the makeshift beds and being safeguarded by the nurse. Fortunately, Hailey is not seriously hurt. She had been able to cover her face after the first two blows from HoJo. Richard walks over to Hailey, who is sitting up in a bed.

"I'm so sorry, Hailey. It's all my fault. I should have just stood up to HoJo earlier on. But James shot him. He's dead. He won't hurt you anymore." He leans over Hailey. "Did he hurt you?".

Hailey does not mention that HoJo attacked her and forced himself on her. She has already blocked that out of her mind. Looking at Richard's bruised and bleeding face, Hailey says, "Richard, you could have been killed. You really stood up to HoJo. I'm so proud of you. But these goons don't care that you're friends with James. They'll kill you." She strokes Richard's face with her hand as Richard closes his eyes.

"Not without it costing their lives. HoJo had it coming." Richard straightens upright.

"Come sit next to me." Richard sits next to Hailey for a moment before again rising. He is really keyed up and his adrenaline still on overdrive.

Hailey sees the blood continuing to flow from the cuts on Richard's face, and she gets up from the bed and moves in closer to stand next to him, as he begins to wobble, losing his balance. "Richard, are you all right?" She holds on to Richard to help him steady himself.

"Thanks, babe." Richard gathers his balance, "Hailey, it's going to be all right. We're free to be with each other. James says so in front of the others after he shot HoJo. You can stay with me in my room from now on without fear."

The nurse walks toward Hailey, but Hailey nods towards her to say she's OK. The nurse stops to take a look at Richard's wounds and motions to Richard to sit on the bed so she can look closer. She takes out some gauze to wipe the blood and examine the cuts on Richard's head. She applies several bandages to the cuts.

Exalted, Hailey smiles and says, "Oh, Richard, now we can be together." She looks lovingly into Richard's eyes. He smiles weakly. "Come here Richard, let me help you. Time to get you home to bed. Nurse, I can take care of him from here," says Hailey.

The nurse nods, handing Hailey some more gauze and bandages. "You're OK to go, Hailey. It doesn't look like you need stitches. Here take some extra supplies," she says.

They leave for Richard's apartment with Hailey wrapping her arms around him, and Richard stumbling along. When they arrive, Hailey opens and closes the door quickly.

Richard cannot wait anymore. He puts his hands around Hailey's waist and pulls her closer to him. "Hailey, I'm in love with you! Spending every day with you is all I think about."

Hailey is also in love with Richard. "I know Richard. I love you, too." Then running her hands through his hair and across his face, she asks, "Richard, you haven't been in many relationships, have you?" He nods.

But she is thrilled that Richard professed his love to her so openly. She has been so touched by his vulnerability.

Richard winces for a second. Then, he does what a man who is thoroughly in love does. He opens up with total honesty. "No, I haven't been in love before, Hailey, not like this. I never really had the time, and it's tough in New York to meet the right someone. All I've ever been able to have are one-night stands. I'm the king of the one-night stands." He laughs. "Go figure I find love in *here*, of all places."

Hailey smiles. "But yes, you now have love, Richard. You're a very special guy, very idealistic, a definite romantic, and you have a big heart. You help people. That's what I love about you." Hailey looks at Richard lovingly. Richard nearly tears up.

Richard is taken aback by Hailey's perceptiveness. "Wow. You got me pegged all right. But you're the most amazing woman I've ever met."

SINFUL LOVE

Hailey says, "Oh, so I'm both your reality and your fantasy? Come, sit next to me on the couch. Let me get the first aid kit and look at those bandages."

Always impressed with Hailey's intelligence, Richard exclaims, "Hailey, yeah, you're both my reality and my fantasy and more!"

Hailey smiles, knowing that she has fallen in love with Richard, she hopes, for the right reasons.

"Come here sit next to me and let me see that nasty cut you got. You took quite a blow to the head. Where did he hit you? Did you black out at all?"

"No, I don't think I have a concussion. I never lost consciousness, though he hit me pretty hard a couple of shots. I'm OK."

Hailey takes Richard's head in her hands and strokes it. "But you kicked his ass! I saw you!"

"Hailey, I love you!" Richard lovingly looks on his beautiful girlfriend as she strokes his face and then kisses him. She notices an additional small cut on the back of his head the nurse must have missed. Hailey takes out a butterfly bandage from the first aid kit and applies it to Richard's cut on the back of his head after first cleaning the wound with gauze and first aid cream. She carefully separates the hair to apply the bandage. Richard also has a couple of bruises as well that Hailey lovingly attends to by kissing them.

Hailey looks at Richard. "Do you really get turned on by getting beat up?" She continues kissing his head where the blood or scars are, over and over, then she locks eyes with Richard and kisses him on the lips and grabs his hand and pulls him to the bedroom.

"Only if it means you'll patch me up! I don't mind all this attention." Richard rises and stumbles a bit still, but now he's really turned on. He looks at Hailey with the hunger of a cougar.

Hailey says, "Hon, we're going to put you to bed. You need some rest. To be continued."

Richard begins to protest, but Hailey walks him over to the bed, undresses him, tucks him in, and then lies next to him, watching him fall asleep. Richard takes a while, fighting his adrenaline, mixed with exhaustion and stress.

"C'mon, Richard, time to sleep! Get some rest, my darling. I will make you go wild in the morning." She gives Richard a look like a lioness before a kill. Richard smiles weakly and then falls asleep.

Hailey then composes herself as the scene with HoJo now plays out in her head, with all the adrenaline now subsided. She undresses and showers to clean herself of the experience, crying softly to herself. The knowledge that HoJo is dead and she will no longer be subjected to the violence and mistreatment gives her the encouragement she needs to get past the incident.

She is grateful to have come out of that experience with little damage to herself and that her man stepped up and risked his life for her to end it. She has never expected her finance guy to be the hero. She looks on at him sleeping next to her and smiles. She is so excited they can be together without any interference.

What's next, she thinks, *is to find a way out of here.*

THE ARRANGEMENTS

The next morning, Richard meets with James Simpson. "James, I want Hailey to stay with me in my apartment and not be subjected to the rest of the posse especially after the HoJo incident. I want to keep Hailey off drugs. I want to be with Hailey solo. I guarantee that this arrangement would not in any way diminish my abilities or focus, but in actuality, it would make them stronger."

Simpson says, "Yo, I already agreed to that. You were too fucked up to hear me say that yesterday. I also know you kept her under wraps all last week. I saw you sneaking food in. And yo, I gotta put her to work somewhere, man. If she's not providing services, she has to do something. No free rides."

Richard pauses, "James, man, you're tough. Look, she's really smart. She can work with me. I need an admin, especially with the new location opening up. I'm going to need some help setting up their books, transitioning to the new team over there. Someone I can trust to oversee them, ongoing. Hailey is a natural leader, a doer. She also has a business background."

Simpson thinks for a moment. "All right. I'll pay her a thousand a week. She's under your watchful eye. Don't make me regret this!"

"You won't regret it, James, thank you. And hey, of course, thanks for saving my ass yesterday. It could have ended bad for me."

"Yo, you know I can't really be seen by the rest of the group as playing favorites with you, in spite of our friendship. I love ya, man. You've done a great job, really. Come here. Give me some love," Simpson says as he and Richard embrace. They make quick eye contact before Richard breaks and strides away quickly.

Richard cannot wait to tell Hailey. He races to his apartment, opens the door. "Hailey, you're here with me. For good!" he says triumphantly. "James said we only have to go to Jamaica to set things up when they're ready and then we can keep an eye on things from here."

She jumps in his arms, kissing him. He picks her up and carries her toward the bedroom, opens the door, and so begins their new stretch of life together. They celebrate by making love.

The more time Richard and Hailey spend together, the closer they become. They finish each other's sentences, get excited when they see each other, and love being together, whether at work or play. Long stares into each other's eyes deepens the smoldering love between them. They eat together, spending lunch together back at the apartment which often leads to passionate lovemaking sessions.

The sex between them gets more deeply passionate and more intimate, loving and caring. Hailey, though small, is fit, strong, and limber and wraps her lithe, small body and legs around Richard in a deep, tight embrace. It is like nothing he has ever experienced.

After they climax repeatedly while in bed, sometimes going until the wee hours of the night, and Richard feels totally spent, Hailey will gently stroke Richard's hair and rub his back and kiss him all over and then starts another cycle. They hold each other tightly after they climax, and Richard gently stokes Hailey all over.

Richard is in heaven. "Oh, my God, you're killing me, Hailey!"

SINFUL LOVE

Hailey took numerous business courses in college in addition to pre law and is a natural in helping Richard with the Den's finances, helping him set up the organizational structure for the new Queens entity. She is smart, disciplined, and thoughtful. The arrangement only serves to further bind them together.

"Hailey, can you—"

"Already done, darling," she says, one step ahead of him.

Richard smiles in acknowledgement.

Hailey marvels at how smart Richard is, and she thinks his financial acumen is genius level.

As much as Richard tries to keep Hailey clean by keeping close to her at all times, Hailey's occasional diversion in still getting high with other Home Girls finally results in Richard breaking protocol. Hailey arrives back at the apartment after sneaking out one night while Richard was napping, catching up on sleep from one of their all-nighter lovemaking sessions. She opens the door quietly. She has forgotten the key. Richard is waiting for her.

"Hailey, where have you been? What are you doing? Wait, are you getting high again? Your eyes are all dilated. Honey, that stuff will kill you!"

Hailey, caught red-handed, is remorseful. "I'm sorry, Richard. I held out as long as I could, but I just can't…can't stop using. That week I was clean with you was amazing, but the crack is like callin' me."

Richard says, "Hailey, we've got to keep you clean. But from now on, you don't go out and party with the girls because those Posse Men are still around, and I don't want you to be with them. Recovery is the only way to get and keep you clean. James knows I want to get and keep you clean. But I don't want him to find out how. I'd rather do this under the radar. I don't want to give him any reason to scrutinize us. I don't really trust anyone around here other than Roger."

The next day, after work, Hailey takes one hit in their apartment from her stash, and it is a frightening scene. She freaks out, having a hallucination that something is eating her skin. Richard is horrified, but he is able to finally calm her down. It is, however, the last straw for Richard to getting Hailey totally clean.

"Hailey, that's it. You have to stop. You can't bring that shit in here! I'm going to help you, baby. I was in Alcoholics Anonymous when I was nineteen. It got me through an excessive period in my life. Now there's Cocaine Anonymous. I know someone who got clean there. We'll go to meetings around here."

"OK, darling, I'll go. But if you were in AA, how come you still drink, Richard?"

"I do, Hailey, but very little. You haven't seen me drink much around here, except with you. I was totally clean and sober for over three years before I started drinking in moderation again. I needed to get through school. There was so much at stake. I learned how to manage it, the alcoholism. I know that's not textbook, but it worked for me as soon as I connected with what I could lose, who I could lose, and I worked the steps to clean a lot of things up. That keeps it real for me every day. I can teach you the twelve-step principles, but you'd be better off going to meetings and learning them firsthand."

He immediately flushes the rest of the drugs down the toilet. Richard knows he has to help Hailey get clean or their arrangement might be in jeopardy if Simpson finds out about Hailey's drugging which can affect her work. Richard is also really worried for her health. Hailey knows it, too. As long as she is on the drug, she knows she can never know peace and clarity.

"Thank you, Richard. I know this is not good. I'll do anything to get clean. I mean it. I know it's a burden to you and to us. I'm sorry."

"Honey, it's no burden to me, I'm worried about you. The next hit could be your last. I love you. I want you to take care of yourself. You're an addict. It's not your fault. The only way to get clean is through a recovery program."

Hailey starts to cry, and Richard pulls her toward him, hold her tightly, and whispers, "It's OK, honey. We're going to get you well. No matter what it takes."

Richard talks about one of his friends at Salomon Brothers who had an addiction to powdered cocaine got clean by attending the twelve-step group Cocaine Anonymous. "It took this guy a while—he kept relapsing—but he did get sober. Problem with cocaine is you either get clean and sober or you die from it. There's nothing in between. You have to get clean, honey."

But how can Richard get Hailey to Cocaine Anonymous meetings while at the Den? James would not allow them to leave to go to meetings where they could possibly talk about the specifics of the Den, even if "what is said in the rooms stays in the rooms." Still, Richard realized there was really no other way to get Hailey clean.

"Simple abstinence isn't the answer," Richard says. "A full-fledged twelve-step program is the only answer to get to the root of the issue. And you need a sponsor, hon, someone in the program with years of sobriety who can talk you through especially the first thirty to ninety days."

"Richard, how can I keep in contact with this sponsor while I'm here?"

Richard whispers to Hailey, "There's a payphone, the only one that works in the building, on the sixth floor by the end of the east wing. I had it fixed awhile back on the QT. The Posse Men do not know it works, not even James. I can sneak you down there to call your sponsor and to call home, too."

"Oh, Richard, that would be amazing if I could just tell Mom I'm OK now with you. I feel like I'm ready to call her now."

"OK, the meeting is at seven PM tomorrow a couple of blocks away. We'll call your parents at in a little while, so we have enough time to double back before Roger notices we're not around," whispers Richard. He then whispers directly in Hailey's ear, "Stuff like this, we need to be careful talking about out loud. I think they may have bugged the apartment."

Hailey nods.

Time has passed, and Richard and Hailey make their way into the lobby of the fifteenth floor.

The Posse Man sentry asks them, "Where are you going?"

Richard says, "just going downstairs to get some air." He is granted access to the elevator with Hailey. They get off on the sixth floor, Richard looks around carefully to make sure they were not followed. They walk to the payphone at the far end of the wing. Hailey is nervous, not having talked to her parents in months. Hailey makes a collect call home. Her mom answers and immediately accepts the charges.

"Mom, It's Hailey."

Her mom screams at the other end. Hailey starts to cry softly.

"I'm so sorry, Mom, for everything. I got caught up with a wrong crowd. I dropped out of school. I got hooked on drugs. But I'm OK now. I met a man, a wonderful man, Mom, who has helped me. He protects me. We're in love. We're in a place that's not good. We're working to get out of here." Hailey looks at Richard. Richard smiles but is not sure how to react.

"Where are you, Hailey? When can we see you? Wait! Your father is here. He wants to talk to you, too. Let me put him on, hold on a moment."

"Hi, Dad. I really miss you."

Hailey's dad got very emotional and repeatedly says, "My baby, my baby."

"We're better get back upstairs, Hailey," says Richard.

"Dad, I love you. I have to go now. I'll call again soon." Hailey tears up as she hugs Richard tightly.

Hailey nods. They walk together hand in hand back to the elevator.

∼

SECRETLY, Richard meets with Roger to discuss his plan to take Hailey to local Cocaine Anonymous meetings to get her sober.

"Roger, I have to get Hailey to meetings at least once a day. It's the only way she'll get and stay clean. I'm not going to lose her like Danielle. I'm in love with her, Roger."

"James will never go for that, Richard. Not even for you."

Richard pauses. "Roger, then we'll have to do this clandestine-like. I need to get Hailey clean and keep her clean. It's not going to work any other way. There's too much temptation at the Den. She needs these meetings. Look, I've made you hundreds of thousands of dollars in your investments, man. Now I'm calling in a favor. It's just an hour or so a day. There are meetings all over the place, some just a couple of blocks away, even. Come on. James still lets me visit my mom with a chaperone once in a while."

"Yeah, I get it, Richard, but that's different. Your visits to your mom are official, part of your agreement with James. If he doesn't agree this time and you do it anyway, we're both fucked."

"That's why he doesn't ever need to know. We go directly, in and out, no stops, no one has to know. Roger, what do you say?"

Roger took a deep breath, and says, "OK, one hour a day. We'll just say we're going for a walk if anyone notices and asks. But it has to be within like three blocks of here. Best time is like in the evening, like six, seven o'clock. We won't be noticed, and we can get away undetected. It's dinnertime. People are eating, and there's a shift change at eight."

"Perfect! That's when most of the meetings are."

Roger says, "Yeah, but be flexible, because if we show a pattern, that will attract attention. We're going to need to mix it up—the days, times, the locations—to make it seem like its less organized."

"Got it. I'll get a meeting list at the first meeting, and we can plot the best days and times and mix them up. Roger, I can't tell you how much this means to me."

"Yeah, I see that Richard. I hope she's worth it."

"She really is. I can see my life rolling out with her."

Roger shakes his head. "This boy is in love." He chuckles. Richard gives him a thumbs up. "You're a lucky guy."

Richard begins to sneak Hailey outside the Den to Cocaine or Narcotics Anonymous meetings in the immediate neighborhood. They both wear hoodie disguises, escorted by his trusted Posse Man friend, Roger. With cocaine addiction at an all-time high in New York City, there is no shortage of meetings and patrons.

It also gave Roger time with Richard, so he could more closely monitor what he and Hailey were doing or talking about as well.

Roger also observed them from time to time at work in the Den. Richard knew he had to be totally careful in justifying Hailey's working with him, but in reality, she really was close to his equal, so it was not a stretch and he didn't care if Roger was watching them, likely at James's behest.

Nothing was more important to Richard than getting Hailey clean. He was very apprehensive about the risk of leaving the complex to go to meetings, but he knew it was the only solution. This had to work.

LIVING WITH SOBRIETY

Soon Hailey has strung ninety days of sobriety together thanks to their clandestine attendance at nearby CA meetings and their twelve-step work together in the apartment. Richard and Hailey are ready to celebrate. Richard invites Roger over to his apartment for the celebration, but he turns them down, not wanting to draw attention.

"I'll hoist one privately for your both. I'm happy for you," he says. They part. Richard and Hailey walk back to their apartment.

Richard and Hailey share a soft drink in celebration, having suspended their drinking of alcohol as part of the twelve-step program's requirements.

Richard congratulates Hailey on the milestone, and they join their soft drink cups in a toast. "Here's to you, Hailey. Great work in getting to ninety days, a huge milestone, because you've turned the corner toward sobriety!"

Hailey kisses Richard strokes his face lovingly, and says, "Richard, you took a big risk for me, you've looked out for me, and you've helped me getting clean. I have loved these last months being with you. You are really special to me. I love you."

Richard tears up a bit. "I love you too, Hailey," he says, choking back the words. "You are remarkable. You did all the hard work.

You're smarter than I am. You really are everything for me. I can't imagine life without you."

Hailey looks at Richard lovingly before kissing him.

∼

OVER THE MONTHS THAT FOLLOW, Richard and Hailey have begun to live a somewhat normal life together in the Den. Richard has shared some of his business acumen with Hailey along with the Den accounting procedures and is pleasantly surprised when she clearly understands and always seems to be one step ahead of him. They work together, eat together, go home to the apartment together, and sleep together, almost in a normal cadence, free from any of the distractions of the Den. The remaining Posse Men are heeding James's mandate not to physically abuse the Home Girls, thanks to Richard's request.

At work, Richard asks for some analytics on one of the offshore accounts, and Hailey, right on the spot, almost instantaneously provides it to Richard with a comment, "It looks a little short in the Cyprus account."

"Wow, you really learn quickly."

"What, you think you're so special, Mr. Finance Hotshot?" Hailey teases, tugging on his shirt collar. "I was a double major in business in undergrad, remember? Pretty soon, I'll be able to do your job!"

Richard is used to being the smartest person in the room, but no more. He has met his match.

Richard shares this with Simpson, and Hailey becomes Richard's full-time, official assistant in overseeing the Den's books, even operations, working alongside Richard's hand-picked bookkeepers.

"James, she's amazing. She picks things up so quickly. I was shocked at her business knowledge. She double majored in business as an undergrad at school," says Richard.

"Yeah, she's super girl. I get it. You lucky sonavagun. You two have some upcoming work to do in Jamaica, too. Want to reorganize things over there."

SINFUL LOVE

Richard and James are sitting together in one of their daily late-afternoon debriefings later that week, discussing the previous day's take and the overall state of the organization's finances. The Den has taken in over one hundred and fifty million dollars in cash in the past twelve months alone, a staggering figure, selling product inventory that sells for a unit price of ten dollars or twenty dollars. But it is so profitable with a margin of over eighty percent even with all the salaries.

Plus, customers buy hundreds of dollars of the drug at a clip as the Den has managed to secure a number of high-profile customers providing exclusive door-to-door delivery service, through beeper contact, and the Den had extremely marketable product names, like Black Diamond, Midnight Blue, along with the best quality stuff on the street.

"Yo, you made the right call, Richard. Your girl is real smart. Just about as smart as you! And you guys did a great job working with the tenants here to get them back on our side. That was huge. Got law enforcement off our backs. To show my appreciation, I'm going to give you another point to up your bonus to six percent of the profits. You can split it with your girl."

"Thanks, James for trusting me. How about seven percent. This way I can give Hailey more than a point. I can give her one of mine, so she'll have three."

James furrows his brow. "Yo, best I can do is 6.25 percent. You work it out. Don't take advantage of my generosity, you get it?" He appreciates his friend's negotiating tactics.

Richard quickly backpedals. "Course not. I can make that work." Richard figures he'll give Hailey 2.25 percent and keep four percent, ever the financial mind. In the end, what will it matter if they are together? For the first time, Richard is seriously thinking about a life that includes Hailey after the Den.

Richard is ecstatic to be around Hailey all day, and they often sneak back to his apartment for lunch and lovemaking. Richard continues to give the rest of the Posse Men investment tips to keep them happy. For most of them, he set up brokerage accounts at his old firm Salomon Brothers and has a former friend there managing the money day to day while Richard makes portfolio tweaks.

Richard and Hailey are in their apartment together. Still thinking that his room is likely bugged, now that he and Hailey are together, Richard as usual, turns on the stereo loud, this time playing Steely Dan's *Aja* CD.

Hailey quietly says, "Richard, can we get out of here? I know we're making money and saving money with your incredible investments for our life ahead, but this is not the life I imagined. I want to get out of here and live a normal life with you. Plus, I haven't seen my family in a year and a half."

"I don't really know if there is a way out, yet." It has crossed his mind to ask Simpson for permission to leave the Den, but he's certain that Simpson will react very negatively and possibly end their current arrangement with a death sentence.

"My singular focus had been on managing the finances, investing, laundering, and hiding the money and the investments in offshore accounts, Hailey. I know these actions are illegal, but I really haven't given myself the opportunity to think beyond the next day. I guess I've become a bit of a machine. I know it's going to end, soon, James says so himself that eventually the Feds will shut us down. It's surprising though that it hasn't already happened. It's already been three years."

"It's because you've made peace with the tenants and given them perks, so they protect James's operation. That was a brilliant move on your part," says Hailey.

"No, it was the right thing to do. The least we could do, improve their living conditions, stop the intimidation."

"And provide great cover for this illegal operation," Hailey counters.

"Yeah, I guess, that, too."

"Richard, what scares me is how easily you've grown accustomed to this life, as a criminal, working for a criminal enterprise."

"Hailey don't call me a criminal. I'm just...just..." Hailey's words sting. For the first time, Richard knows she is right. Stricken, he sits on the couch and buries his head in his hands.

"Richard, I'm sorry. I didn't mean that. You're a good man." Hailey sits down next to Richard and puts her arms around him and kisses him. "You just got caught up in this. You've made a tremendous difference here. The Home Girls are treated better now, the tenants got some real improvements, you invest for the Posse Men, and you've made everyone's life better here in spite of this criminal enterprise. But it has to end, and it's time for us to move on with our lives." Hailey looks Richard dead in the eye.

"Richard, you need to start thinking about *our* life after the Den. You really need to come to terms with what we're doing here. It's wrong and immoral. We're helping a drug cartel get rich off of people's misery, largely my people—African American people. Can't you see that? Doesn't that bother you?"

Richard goes to hug Hailey close, kisses her, and whispers, "Yes, of course, it bothers me. I know it's especially hard on black people. I know it's immoral, and I want it to end, too. Hailey, keep your voice down, honey. We have to be careful what we say out loud. They might have hidden cameras in here. Smile, so they think I'm whispering something funny."

Hailey smiles, but frowns on the inside. Through grinning teeth, she whispers, "If you're the man I love, you'll get us out of here and do something to shut this thing down." She turns away from Richard to make the point.

It is like a mortal wound for Richard to hear, but he takes it. "Yes, I will. And I am...the man you love. I will do the right thing, Hailey, I promise you." Richard then responds loudly over the stereo, for all to hear, "Yes, it's a good life here, Hailey. I like working here. Hey, let's take a shower together."

Richard then grabs Hailey gently by the arm and leads her into the bathroom. Richard knows there are no cameras or bugs in the tiny bathroom because he has examined the room himself and the bathroom is sparsely laid out. They can continue their discreet conversation there.

"Honey, come with me." Hailey frowns and agrees, following Richard toward the bathroom.

Richard and Hailey enter the bathroom and remain in their clothes outside the shower stall. To be sure, Richard turns the shower on and says softly to Hailey, as they sit on the toilet seat together. "Hailey, you don't understand. This place is like the Mafia. Once you're in, you can't get out unless they kill you. But I know James won't do this forever. He's got like a four-year plan or something and he's like three years or more into it. Eventually the cops or the Feds will shut him down, and he knows it. That's the time we run."

Hailey looks at Richard, disappointed, and replies, "Four-year plan? How can you even be sure he'll let you just walk away? Richard, you know too much. You're a liability. Think about that one. Do you want to live the rest of your life looking over your shoulder? Richard, I don't want to be here two more hours, let alone two more months, let alone another year. I don't care how comfortable we are. Don't you care what Simpson is doing to people? What we're doing—selling those drugs to people—it's immoral. It's wrong. You need to take a stand! People are dying from it. It's offensive, and I won't be part of it anymore. You need to call on the authorities to shut this down."

Richard nods, "Yes, yes, Hailey, you're right." He looks at Hailey and says under his breath, "Hailey, but we have to be careful about openly talking about this. That kind of talk will get us in trouble or even killed around here if someone overhears us."

Hailey challenges Richard. "Richard, I don't want to be here anymore, ruining people's lives like this. I was going to law school to uphold the law, not to break it and certainly not so that a drug lord can make millions while people kill themselves and ruin other people's lives. You need to make a decision. You used to be a man of principle. I get it that you made a mistake, out of financial survival or something and you saw a money-making opportunity. But this isn't you. I know that. You help people, not hurt people. That's not the man I fell in love with. What about your soul?"

Richard pauses for a long time. "You're right. I have…have not been true to myself. I sold out because I needed the money. But I know now I can no longer do this. I've had the blinders on for so long. I felt dead inside, Hailey, like nothing mattered. Until I met you. You've changed everything. Now you've given me a reason to live again."

"Yes, but now, my love, you have something, someone that matters, your life, my love, our love, our life together. I want our lives back. I want to live a normal life with you. Get us out of here and shut this down for us, for everyone, not just me."

"You win, honey. OK, I just need to figure out how to get us out of here. It won't be easy. I need to think, plan this out."

"Let me help you," Hailey says.

"It's better if I don't tell you. If they ever become suspicious, they can't pit us against each other because you won't know anything. Let me do the thinking for both of us now."

Sure enough, Hailey replies, "OK, if you must."

Richard and Hailey have talked about life together after the Den before, but this is the first time Hailey has been so forceful, almost to the point of issuing an ultimatum to Richard. It's clear to Richard that he has to make a getaway plan. No more time for being comfortable.

He thinks, *how can he lie to himself and Hailey forever and keep the status quo?* That is no longer an option now that Hailey has given him something to fight for—her and their love. But her knows his love's principles and his own mean he had to do the uncomfortable thing, the right thing. How is he going to get them out of there and end the run of James Simpson?

Just then there is a knock at the door. A stern voice is heard from behind the it. "All right, you lovebirds, time to come out."

Richard turns off the shower, goes to open the door, and it is James Simpson. Richard lets him in to the vestibule. Hailey, playing the part smartly, walks out of the bathroom in her robe with a towel on her head.

Simpson looks Hailey up and down. "Damn, Richard, you're a lucky man. Come on, there's a meeting with everybody in ten minutes in Apartment 15A, main room to go over the new Jamaica operation. Let's go. I need you both."

Richard says, "OK. Give us five minutes to get dressed, and we'll be there, James."

"Aw right," James walks out, winking at Richard.

Hailey gets dressed quickly and they leave a few minutes later.

The meeting is about the finalization of the logistics of the new Jamaica Crack Den operation. James's plan is to relocate a portion of the staff from each area at the Harlem location to Jamaica and is initially asking for volunteers before he assigns people. Richard and Hailey know they will have to make a trek out there once or twice a week to check in on whichever accounting person from the Den is assigned to relocate there, but otherwise they will remain at the Harlem location.

Since not enough volunteers agree to relocate to Jamaica, James then dictates who is to move over there to a cavalcade of groans.

"Fucking Jamaica? That's Queens," is overheard being said by the workers. "Them crazy Jamaicans over there," is also heard.

Simpson is having none of it. "Whoever doesn't want to go, that's fine. I have a body bag for you. You get my drift? Say the fuckin' word." After that, there are no protests.

"Richard and Hailey, I want you both there nine AM Monday morning to set things up, you dig? Mookie see that they have safe transport. That's it. Dismissed. Now go back and pack my product and do yo thing!"

Richard and Hailey nod, but for the first time, it is with reservation that they keep to themselves as they make eye contact. They know their future is at stake to somehow find a way out of the Den. They both realize that there will be anxious moments ahead awaiting them.

COMING CLEAN

Now with each passing moment, Richard and Hailey are talking about life after the Den. After the meeting with James, their conversations draw them to talking about each other. They continue to declare their love for one another, and they need to find a way out of the den. Richard preaches patience and timing. They even talk about how many children they want to have together. They agree to have two for starters.

"But you have to finish law school first, honey,"

"After that, I want your children, Richard." It sends chills up and down Richard's spine. He is never heard those words before, and he knows there's no turning back with Hailey. She is a woman who knows what she wants.

After dinner, Richard and Hailey go to a Cocaine Anonymous meeting several blocks away in the basement of Salem United Methodist Church on 129th. Roger escorts them but waits outside the room, not wanting to be seen by anyone in the group. Richard introduces himself as a recovering alcoholic, and he is welcomed at any other twelve-step program.

The meeting starts, and soon Hailey raises her hand to share. It is one of the handful of times she has shared during the now four plus months she has been attending the meetings. She has not wanted to draw much attention to herself.

"Hi, my name is Hailey, and I am an addict. I have one hundred and thirty-three days sober. I wouldn't be here except for the courage and encouragement of my boyfriend, Richard," she starts, looking toward Richard fondly. Richard smiles weakly as Hailey touches his arm. "I know we talk about not having relationships with the opposite sex for one year into our sobriety, but Richard is a twelve-step program graduate and is my life sponsor as well as my love.

"I'm not suggesting anyone else do this. It just works for me. Now that I have achieved some sobriety and worked the first three steps, it is clear to me that the situation my boyfriend and I are in is the most unhealthy, unsavory, and dangerous place to be. We have a problem that we need to find our way out of, but I trust this man with all of my heart to figure out a way out of this for us so we can have the life together we both deserve. Right now, I'm scared because the future is so uncertain. But I'm optimistic we will figure it out. I just know, no matter what, I'm going to stay sober. Thank you. I'm Hailey, and I'm an addict."

The room claps.

One older white woman, Stephanie, Hailey's sponsor for the past three months, motions toward Hailey and calls out quietly across to her, "I'm so proud to be your sponsor."

Having been around drugs and the addictive Den atmosphere, it has been uncomfortable at times for Richard at the CA meetings, as it reminds him of his teenage alcoholism and the AA meetings, and finally in this CA meeting he breaks down and shares. Surprisingly, perhaps inspired by Hailey's share, Richard raises his hand and is selected next to share.

"Hi, I'm Richard, and I am an addict. This isn't working. I need to come clean. I'm working for one of the largest crack dealers in New York, and I can't take it any more being surrounded by the violence and misery all day, that I'm partially responsible for.

"I'm enabling it to happen, contributing to people getting addicted and dying. It's going to kill me, ruin my life, and all that is important to me, the guilt. I'm in such pain. I've medicated on making numbers work my entire time there, but I've been ignoring my responsibilities as a human being. This is not who I am. I help people, not hurt them. I need to make this right and somehow end this. Get away from it, shut it down. I just don't know how," he rambles on.

After a long pause, Richard concludes, "I'm Richard, and I'm an addict."

There is a dead silence. Then after about fifteen seconds, a few claps then a crescendo of clapping and then a standing ovation. Richard has his head in his hands. Hailey has put her arms around him and then takes his head in her hands and rotates his head to kiss him. Richard blinks and smiles back. Then fear gripped him. What if Roger overheard?

Richard cannot believe what he just confessed out loud, but at this point, he knows there's no turning back. He immediately looks to the back of the room to see if Roger is in the room, and exhales when he sees he is not. But Roger is standing against the door, from the outside, listening in and heard every word.

Verbalizing his intentions fuels Richard with the strength to take the next steps to set him and Hailey free.

After the meeting is over, Richard and Hailey know they are not to linger, so they leave immediately. Roger is waiting in the lobby of the church and asks, "How did the meeting go?"

Richard mumbles, "Good. Hailey got to share. She has one hundred and thirty-three days,"

"That's good. OK. Let's hustle back," said Roger, not revealing he had overheard Richard's share of their escape plan.

And they walk quickly in the night back to the Den. Roger has his own dilemma. Does he confront Richard to dissuade him from attempting something that could endanger his and Hailey's life, or does he report it directly to James? Richard notices the silence from Roger and his Spider-Man sense is tweaked. He says nothing.

Meanwhile, Roger is thinking about his options. If he reports what he heard to James, he feels, not only could James eliminate both Richard and Hailey, but it will also not bode well for Roger that he has been allowing them to go to meetings outside of the Den for the past four plus months. So, for now, Roger is going to sit on it. But his loyalties are split, compromised by the fear for his own life. It is not a good place to be. He wished he had never overheard Richard's share at the meeting. He realizes that soon he will have to take a stand.

Maybe, he thinks, *Richard will listen to reason and back down.*

Later, Hailey and Richard are discussing the meeting in his apartment with the music up loud as a cover. Richard says, "I don't know why I shared what I did. It just came out. What if Roger overheard? He was really quiet after the meeting. That's not like him. I'm not sure now."

"Richard, what you shared took a lot of guts. But we must be extra careful. You don't know who you can trust around here or not. James's violent tendencies can transcend loyalty or friendship. We have to assume we can't trust anyone, including Roger. He could have been listening in. You're right."

Richard nods. "Do you know about Roger? He was an engineering student at Cornell. His parents live in Harlem. His dad got really sick a few years back, and he had to return to the city to help out. He's a real smart guy. Roger was one of James's best friends going way back to the 'hood. Roger has a strong moral compass, too. We spent many a night talking during our early days here, about how we were going to help James out for a stretch, make some money for our families and then get out. But we haven't had that conversation for a long time. Roger got just as sucked up into this vortex, and I did, too. But I think we can turn him."

"Richard, no. Please, you can't trust anyone. Even Roger. James must have something on him to hold over him. That's how it works. Don't make Roger choose between you and James. You will lose."

Richard, marveling at how clairvoyant Hailey is, smiles at his love. "How did you come to that conclusion?"

"Richard, honey, I read people. It's part of being a good lawyer.

Roger is a great guy. I just don't think he's in a position to help us with James and he knows it. Just by helping us already, he's put himself in a bind. If James ever finds out he's been taking us to meetings that would not be good. No, you can't tip your hand with Roger. That would be a mistake, trust me."

"What if he brings it up, that he overheard my share at the meeting and that we want out,"

"Just say, it was something you said out of frustration, in the moment, but that you'll see this thing through. You know, it was a mistake, a temporary lapse in judgement."

"Should I volunteer that?"

"No," says Hailey, "let him come to you if he's going to. He may not. I know it will be awkward, but you need to put on your game face. If he doesn't come to you, we know where he stands."

"I can do that," says Richard, who adds, "Then I better be super careful, take my time planning this. Can't rush it."

Hailey nods, though in her gut she wants out of there tomorrow. "*Our* time," she looks at her man.

PLANNING THE ESCAPE

Richard begins to plot their escape from the Crack Den. He does not even share the details with Hailey, to protect her. Richard knows Simpson will never let him leave the Crack Den and the business unless he has leverage over him. Simpson always said the only way out was in a body bag.

Richard figures he has to determine a way to move some of the den's offshore accounts to another set of unmarked offshore accounts as leverage for their escape. But he has to do so without knowing where the money was moved to, so Simpson cannot torture him for the new account information.

How can he get that leverage? He clearly needs outside help, he figures, as he cannot possibly trust anyone in the Den to help pull this off.

He concludes will ultimately need to enlist the help of his former banker/trader friend and running mate, Brian Lowenstein from his Salomon Brothers days, who he figures can have the offshore accounts setup through an intermediary, while maintaining the access codes in a safe, inaccessible place, so that Richard can make his play to escape the Den, to ensure his and Hailey's safety. Richard and Lowenstein have explored setting up offshore accounts while at Salomon Brothers on behalf of certain clients, so they knew the mechanics of it. Richard fondly remembers those days as well as the abundance of one-night stands they had together and the comparing of notes. Lowenstein was able to get Richard to get out of his shell and go out with women. There is no one Richard trusts more than his friend Brian Lowenstein.

As long as Richard does not know the codes, Richard thinks, *he has leverage.* But if something goes wrong and Simpson figures out his move? Richard knows he must have a contingency plan.

If anything happens to Richard, he figures, he can threaten that the codes will be anonymously turned over to the FBI along with a lot of other incriminating evidence.

No, mentioning or threatening to go to the FBI will surely get him killed, he corrects himself.

How about the money will be dispersed to various charities automatically? *That is real leverage,* he thinks, *plus it would kill James to think his money was going to charity.* It seems like the workings of a perfect plan.

Richard's ultimate outcome is to give Simpson the codes once he and Hailey are both safely away. By not actually knowing the codes nor who has them, Simpson cannot force the information out of him or Hailey and would be forced to let them go, Richard figures.

Richard knows he has to work right under the noses of the bookkeepers he himself hired and trained because they also have access to the same offshore accounts. Richard will have to move the funds to the new temporary accounts and then give access to those accounts to Lowenstein's contact to move the money to the new accounts during a brief window and hope it goes unnoticed. He will need to move the money to those temporary accounts at the exact time Richard needs to make his escape. And he needs to do this all undetected.

It is risky, but it seems like the formation of a good plan. What about mice and men? Once Richard and Hailey are both safely away and in route to the foreign destination of their choice—maybe Spain or Greece?—he will then drop an anonymous tip to the FBI with all the gory details. The Den and James Simpson would be history after the FBI raids the Den, he figures.

Richard's escape plan is to get as far away from the Posse Men's eyes as possible to start his escape, meet Hailey at a rendezvous point with an easy escape point from the Den, going down the back staircase at the far extreme end of the east building end of the complex out to the street. That way they can escape, undetected, from the street and get away in a cab to meet Lowenstein at a remote place and then they would all leave for JFK airport together. It all seemed easy.

From the airport just before they board their flight, he would plan to contact Lowenstein to reach out to his connections in the Caribbean to provide the access codes which Richard would then phone into Simpson to complete the negotiation for his and Hailey's safety. If anything goes wrong and they do not get a clean getaway, Richard figures he still has enough of an upper hand to negotiate their safe passage. James is just into the money and will maintain a cool head as long as he gets his codes back with all the money intact, Richard surmises.

Richard has still not told Hailey any of the details. He has told her, time and again, over her protests, the less she knows, the better.

They are sitting together in the apartment in the kitchen at the small bistro table, running the water in the sink nearby to provide some audio cover.

"Richard," she whispers, "please let me help you."

"Hailey, it's better if you don't know the details. Plausible deniability, you know."

Hailey finally agrees in resignation. "Why? Because I'm a lousy liar!"

"No kidding. You're going to be an attorney. You can't lie, right?"

"Yes, when I get out of here, when *we* get out of here, it's straight back to law school. Then, I'm going to open my own law firm. I decided I would do that during undergrad. A group of us pledged to come together to practice law together after law school. To change how blacks are being treated and represented in the legal system. It's disgraceful and un-American. There is no justice for them."

Richard nods.

"Richard, what do you want to do when you—I mean we—get out of here?"

Richard thinks for a moment and a chill comes down his spine when he realizes he does not really have an answer. He has shut off that part of his brain, his heart, for so long by becoming James Simpson's right hand and chief financial officer. He has literally parked his soul.

Now, he pauses and lets that really sink in, and a "what was I thinking?" speaks to him in judgement inside his head. He immediately becomes present to his predicament and it hits him like a roundhouse punch. He feels it in his stomach literally. He nearly collapses, having to catch himself, and he looks away from Hailey, who reads him like a book, seeing the pain in his body and his soul. She immediately comes to his rescue, holding on to him to steady him.

"Richard, I know you once had dreams, dreams to help people. You just lost track of that in here. I know. It's all right. Let it go. We both made mistakes. But I know you want to right things when we get out of here and back in the real world again. I know that's important to you. Because I know you. You're the most generous, noble man I know."

"Hailey, stop saying that," Richard begins bitterly. "I'm a fraud. I'm a liar. You're right. I *am* a criminal. The only thing I'm good at is accelerating people's misery. I don't...I don't know if there's hope for me." The words sting and surprise Richard.

"Richard don't say that," Hailey leans in close to Richard and takes his head in her gentle hands and she pulls him toward her, so he is an inch away from her face. She looks in his eyes and sees the pain and the sadness that Richard can never keep from her. She strokes his face, wipes a tear away. She kisses him all in one motion.

"You are a good man. Stop feeling sorry for yourself. Yes, you made a mistake, but you thought you were helping an old friend. You can turn this around. I believe in you. I will help you. I'm here for you. Don't think about where you are right now or how you got here, think back, think back about what was important to you. Remember that. It's still there, Richard," Hailey says and then kisses Richard for a long moment. They embrace, and Richard goes limp in Hailey's arms.

"Hailey, I love you. You give me, such, such strength. God bless you." Richard kisses Hailey back, and after a long pause, staring into Hailey's eyes, he clears his throat to speak. Hailey stares back into Richard's eyes with an intensity he has not felt before.

"I used to want to help people, everyday people, people who didn't have an investor's background, to teach them the importance of investing the right way and to plan early for their legacy, their retirement. I was never interested in making rich people richer. After I lost my job on Wall Street with the crash, I gave advice to family and friends on how and when to get into the market, where to invest. I gave my mother and sister some money to invest in the market to get them started in the market after the crash, which is actually the best time to invest because stock prices are at their lowest. You know what, I'll open a non-profit organization or something, teaching people how to invest, some way to give back. I guess I can really open any business I like. As long as it serves a purpose, the greater good."

"And we'll do that together, darling. You will need a good lawyer after all!" says Hailey. Richard brightens and smiles back at Hailey and mouthed "I love you."

He gets up, smiles back at Hailey, and says, "Honey, I've got something I have to do. I'll be back before too long," he says as he kisses Hailey.

"Be careful," Hailey looks into Richard's eyes and grabbing his hands with hers. Richard smiles and walks out.

∼

RICHARD SNEAKS AWAY to the sixth floor to make a call on the payphone. He makes sure he is not followed. The only working phone with an outside line in the Den is in James Simpson's office, under lock and key.

He had asked one of tenants he had befriended on the floor to call a private contractor to do so under the radar. The tenant snuck the repairperson in with a food delivery to do his dirty work. Richard was the king of secret activities. Somehow, he knew the need to make outside calls out of sight would be necessary.

He gets to the phone, drops a quarter in, and dials. "Ben! Thank God you're there. OK tell me about everything. Is it all set?" Richard says. "Great. OK, let's roll the dice. It's going to be next Tuesday night. Be ready. I'll call you at four PM that day to confirm. I'll move the money at exactly five thirty PM so be ready. Yeah, the two of us. Thanks, bro."

Richard could not hide his excitement nor his anxiety over the days to come. Next Tuesday could not come soon enough.

D DAY

It is a cold January morning in 1992. New York City's mayor, David Dinkins continued to oversee a city besieged in drugs and criminal activity. In many ways, a new era is upon the country and New York City as the crack epidemic eventually does fizzle out.

The nationwide war on drugs is about to explode and continues to fill the prisons with African American youths. The increased law enforcement pressure that is beginning to make some inroads on crack operations in New York City, driving many crack operations to the suburbs and rural areas to unprepared law enforcement.

Their clock radio goes off, blasting the alarm in the background. Richard wakes Hailey up gently. "Hailey, honey, this is the day. Like we planned," he whispers, kissing Hailey to wake her up. It is 6:00 AM. The sun is starting to peek through the horizon in their bedroom window, through the curtains which faced east toward Spanish Harlem. Richard had long ago opened the curtains nailed to the windows to let the sun in at Hailey's request. He does not care of James approved or not.

"OK, I'm ready. Richard, try not to get too excited. Play it cool. You got this." She kisses Richard and looks him in the eyes.

Richard feels slightly agitated but ready to execute his plan. "Just how we discussed it again last night, honey. We meet back here after our shift is over and make our way out. Take what we have packed. If I'm not back here by 5:45 PM, you leave and meet me at the rendezvous place."

Hailey nods, she and Richard having gone over this numerous times in the past week.

"Just like the dry run we did last Tuesday," Richard recalls, when they easily made it to their rendezvous point undetected and scaled down the internal stairs all the way to the street level door, which was alarmed but shut off. It was almost too easy.

Through the door's window, Richard had detected numerous cabs at the corner nearby and knew the nearby Apollo Theatre would have many cabs queued up for their escape. It seemed almost too easy during the dry run. They both had remarked that they had wished they would have kept going, but Richard had not moved the money or taken his insurance policy, the financial records with him.

It is now the evening, after 5:00 PM. Richard is ready to go. He has clandestinely packed the laptop from his office in his messenger bag while no one was looking. Richard had convinced James to allow him to use a laptop, so he would be more portable in a pinch, in case they have to move the data fast and the built-in floppy disk with only 1.44MB of storage would not hold enough for larger files. It is a typical smart move for Richard that will now pay off as newer laptops in the 1990s allowed for more hard drive storage.

Richard accesses the off shore accounts from his laptop but he is only able to transfer fifty million of the total 150 million dollars that should have been in the current offshore accounts to the temporary offshore account to be accessed through a third party by Brian Lowenstein. For fleeting moment, Richard thinks about calling it off, that maybe James is on to him, but there is no way he is going through with this. He has to since he has already transferred the funds out from the Den's offshore accounts to the accounts setup by Lowenstein which will be noticed soon by his accounting team at the den.

Something does not sit right. Where was the other hundred

million dollars unaccounted for from the Den's offshore accounts that was there when he accessed them earlier in the day? *Who moved the funds?* he wondered.

He nervously arrives at the apartment at 5:40 PM. But where is Hailey? She is supposed to meet him there in the apartment, so they can leave together. He remembers plan B. If Richard cannot make it back to their apartment on the fifteenth floor by 5:45PM, Hailey is to leave and to meet Richard by the back staircase of the east wing building on the eighth floor, their rendezvous place. He told her to make sure she was not followed. Maybe Hailey left early, before him. Why would she do that, break from the plan?

Richard is fighting panicking. *What if Hailey did not get away? What if they got to her first? This is their only window of opportunity to leave,* he thinks. She must have gotten away, he corrects himself. If he does not go now, not only will he be caught in his plot, but also Simpson may just shoot him and Hailey. However, he remembers that as long as the codes are safely with Lowenstein's offshore handler, he has leverage. And the only way he is able to contact Lowenstein is in person at the Brooklyn Battery terminal where he and Lowenstein have planned an escape route by boat. Suddenly, Richard is steely again. Even if he was only able to transfer $50 million dollars, it should be enough he figures.

Richard leaves his apartment and runs into Roger walking down the hallway toward the front of the apartment.

Roger says, "Where are you going?"

Richard looks away. "Nowhere, just going to pick up my food delivery." He nervously tucks his bag with his laptop under his arm, hoping Roger did not notice.

Roger looks at him and nods. He sees the bag under Richard's arm, but does not acknowledge it. "OK. Be cool, brother."

Richard looks back at him and continues on. Roger continues to walk toward the main apartment. Richard walks in the direction of the elevator bank as if to meet the food deliveryman who would have been cleared by the Posse Man station in the lobby that controls all traffic in and out of the building. He is now out of Roger's sight.

Richard spins around, notices he is alone, and then darts down the far end of the hallway where he begins his journey to the emergency staircase at the extreme end of the building. Richard enters the staircase and then makes his way down to the eighth floor, where he begins to see that Simpson, three Posse Men, and Hailey are all waiting for him on the platform of the stairs. Hailey, knowing it is Richard, calls up to him before he is visible, "Richard, run!"

Too late, Richard gets to the eighth-floor staircase platform and is surprised to see Simpson and the others.

Roger is with him, holding Hailey. He nods at Richard as if to say, "Gotcha." Now Richard figures Roger must have told James about their plan, overhearing them from the CA meeting. He must have somehow figured out today was the day by spying on them after the CA meeting and followed Richard after they met at the elevator bank and radioed to Simpson. In fact, Roger was shadowing him ever since the CA meeting.

"Hailey, are you all right? So, this is how it is, Roger?" says Richard.

"I'm sorry, Richard. They were waiting for me at the apartment and brought me here," said Hailey.

Simpson says, "Going somewhere? What do you think? I didn't know you were leaving. My boy Roger here told me of your master plan to escape and figured out your rendezvous place here. He's been following you, fool."

Richard takes a deep breath, composes himself. "Look, James, I would have come to you with my request to leave. But I know it wouldn't have made a difference, and you would have said no. Man, this is not a place for me and Hailey anymore. But I knew you wouldn't just let us go."

Simpson says, "You're right, I wouldn't have let you go. But you could have just talked to me. We could have figured something out. We're going to shut down soon anyway. You could have just waited!"

"Yeah, with us looking over our shoulders the rest of our life. No, thanks. James, I'm not looking to hurt anyone here, you know that. You gave me an opportunity—us an opportunity—which I greatly appreciate, and in return I made you a lot of money and safeguarded your money."

"Oh, you mean the $50 million you stole? You did what you were paid to do, nothing more. I'm not running a fucking nonprofit and shit here. You were well-paid and now you stab me in the back?" He is turning bright red. "You are a fucking turncoat. You think I let my guard down just because I let you and your ho sleep together? You were my friend! I saved your fucking life! I should have let HoJo shoot your ass! Search him!"

Richard hands over the messenger bag and puts his arms in the air. Roger pats him down, finding nothing. Roger opens the bag and shows the laptop to James. Richard exhales because he had already removed the laptop's tiny hard drive with all his files and had taped it between his butt cheeks, undetected.

"James, I am not doing it for the money. I…we…just want out. All I want is to leave with me and Hailey. You don't have to worry about me going to the police or FBI because I don't want to do time, either. They're going to figure out I did the books here. Nor would I *ever* rat on you, James, you know that."

Simpson is furious, though he almost appreciates his friend's dilemma, but nonetheless is *not having it*. "You won't tell the FBI? Fuck, you don't think I've never heard of cutting an immunity deal. Is that what you have planned for me, you fuck?"

Richard hands Simpson a transition plan document he had prepared, where he outlines all of the processes, procedures, accounts. "Everything you need, everything, printed out, and all my files are on your network. You know I cross-trained the lead bookkeeper and his staff members to be able to do whatever has to be done in my absence. Everything clicks like clockwork. You don't need me or Hailey."

"James, let us go. Richard has left you with every detail. We just want to get on with our lives. We wish you no harm. Let us live our lives. That used to mean something to you, didn't it?"

James, furious, walks over to Richard with the gun in his hand and waves it at Richard. Richard does not flinch.

"James, I knew you would never let us leave, so I had to have my own contingency plan."

Simpson scowls.

"I have transferred the fifty million dollars from the offshore accounts and a third party, who I do not know, are holding this money for me. I will give you the account numbers only after we are safely away."

Two of the Posse Men move toward Richard menacingly, their guns waved out. But Simpson waves off the Posse Men.

Richard says, "If any harm comes to me or Hailey and I don't meet my contact in the next sixty minutes, the money will be gone for good. It will be donated to a gazillion untraceable charities. I won't be able to retrieve it. I don't want that to happen. Just let us go and I'll go and get the new codes and call you with them."

"What is this shit? You're trying appeal to my business interests and our friendship and shit? Too late for that! And now you're trying to extort me for *my* money? What the fuck?" bellows Simpson.

Richard again appeals to Simpson. "I just want out for me and for Hailey so we can start a life together. We'll disappear together, I swear."

Simpson then strikes Richard across the ear with the gun butt, knocking Richard to the ground and says, "Oh, you want to start your life together, eh? Fucking start this! Did you really think that when you relocated the fifty million dollars, we weren't paying attention? The money was moved by you at five thirty PM this evening. I had your team watching out for alerts they put on for transactions and shit. I was wondering when you were going to come to me with an explanation after you moved the money. We moved over a hundred million to different accounts earlier in the day because I didn't trust you. Damn, I never figured you would use the fifty million for an exit strategy."

Richard rises slowly with blood trickling down his face. Hailey makes a move toward him, but Roger snaps her back.

"Ow, you're hurting me, Roger."

Roger says nothing and does loosen his grip.

Simpson looks at Richard and says, "Are you stupid enough to think I trusted you with full control of all of our investments? I had one of your lieutenants move the other hundred million dollars right behind your back. He was watching *my money*. I didn't think you'd go for the bait. Shit." Simpson, still burnishing the gun, sticks it in Richard's face.

Richard says, "Yeah, but if you want to see that fifty million again, you let us go. One hour, James. If I don't meet my connection in one hour—now fifty-seven minutes—the money's gone for good. You let us pass safely, you'll get your money back. I'm not extorting you or blackmailing you. I'm doing this for love, James. Once I get the codes, I'll park it in another account and send you the details. Isn't sparing my life and Hailey's life, worth fifty million dollars to you? We'll leave New York, and you'll never see or hear from us again."

Simpson is still furious. "I'm going to tell you what *my* real leverage is. Your girl. She *stays*. You get to leave town for good once you give me back the rest of my money from your connection. But I'm holding on to your girl, man. Afterward, I don't want to see you anywhere *near* New York for the next, like, five or ten years and shit. If I do, or if anyone I know smells your filthy breath from miles away, not only will I kill you, but your girl here dies. That is if I don't decide to put you in a body bag right here for this stunt! She stays here as long as I keep her. If you try to do *anything* to get her out, she dies. Don't even think about calling the FBI. She dies! Now go and get me those account codes before I change my mind and kill you both here right now. If I don't hear back from you in sixty minutes with those codes, you both die!"

Richard stammers, "No, that's not the deal, James. Hailey comes with me or you can kiss the fifty million dollars goodbye."

James fires his pistol just over Richard's head. Richard ducks. "There's my answer!"

"Roger, take June Bug and Roy here and this piece of shit to wherever he's meeting his connect and make sure you come back with those account codes. Then call me when you have them," Simpson demands. "After that, take him to the airport and watch him board a plane."

Richard stammers, "No, no, you can't do that! Hailey comes with me! If I don't contact my partner in sixty minutes and we aren't *both* safe, those investments will be permanently gone. I don't have a phone number, just a location. If we both don't show up, your money's gone."

Simpson yells, "You are in no position to make any demands. Get the *fuck* out of here. Meet your man to release the rest of *my* money, or you're both dead. *Go!* Before I decide to fuck the fifty million dollars and kill you both for fun right here. The bitch stays, you got that?"

With that, Simpson swings his gun and strikes Richard across the face again, his blood splattering. Hailey pushes off Roger and runs to Richard, wiping the blood off his face. Roger then walks back over to her and grabs her by the arm again, this time waving the gun at Hailey. Hailey spits in his eye. Roger wipes it off but does not strike her.

Richard, kneeling, looks back at Simpson through blood-stained eyes and says finally, "James, if I give you the codes, you have to promise no harm comes to Hailey. She has nothing to do with this. It was all me. Promise me. And then you'll let her go."

Simpson, perplexed, but realizing Richard's real motivation is to protect his woman once again, replies, "You are one *fucked up* dude, man. You risk all this, for what, freedom? I told you it was only a matter of time anyway before we would have to shut down and take our cut. Why couldn't you just wait? I loved you, man! Like a brother! We could have rode this to the end if you just waited! Then you go and pull this shit." Simpson is emotional. "Now get the fuck going!"

Hailey looks at Richard. "Richard, what's happening? You said you would take me with you! You said this would work. Don't leave me behind with these animals. Richard! Richard!"

"Say goodbye to your bitch, chump." Simpson then breaks into a huge laugh.

Richard is frozen, feeling a knife penetrating his heart as he looks into Hailey's eyes as he hears Hailey's voice trail off followed by Simpson's laugh. His gaze is frozen in anguish.

Realizing his window of opportunity and his leverage was diminishing, Richard walks to Hailey, hugs her tightly against him, and whispers, "Hailey, I'm so sorry, I screwed up. It was supposed to be both of us leaving, but James must have found out about my plan. I'll come back for you somehow. I love you with all my heart."

Hailey is obviously shaken and whispers the words, "I love you" into Richard's ear. They are abruptly pulled apart by Simpson who pushes Richard in the direction of the staircase going down, and Richard stumbles down the first two or three stairs before righting himself, with Roger hot on his tail with the two other Posse Men.

~

Richard leaves the building with Roger and the other two Posse Men, hopping in a yellow cab to meet Lowenstein.

"Where are we going?" barks Roger at Richard.

"The Brooklyn Army Terminal," says Richard in the general direction of the driver. They should have just enough time to get there if the BQE will cooperate. Richard tells the driver, "Brooklyn Army Terminal, Building C, like Charlie, step on it. There's an extra twenty in it for you if you make it in under forty minutes." The driver happily smiles.

Posse man June Bug shows the driver the gun menacingly. The

SINFUL LOVE

driver peels off the curb and hits the accelerator towards the Harlem River Drive, several blocks east.

Richard rides in the front of the cab. He has one more contingency up his sleeve. Richard has worked out with Lowenstein that in case he and Hailey are in trouble or being followed, or the plan was compromised, that they would arrive in a car in front Building C at the Brooklyn Army Terminal. On the flipside, if Richard and Hailey were let off at the adjacent Building D, Lowenstein knew that everything went according to plan, and they got away undetected. Lowenstein would be stationed inside Building C at the rear of the lobby out of sight where he could see which building Richard and Hailey would be left off in front of to play out his hand.

Richard fumbles for the map of the plan he drew up of the BAT inside the front seat of the cab to give it a quick glance of Building C and the complex, out of the view of the three Posse Men in the back seat. He knew he needed to somehow get sufficient separation from the Posse Men during the chaos Lowenstein was planning to get enough of a lead on them to escape by boat, especially since they had guns. His heart was racing.

Richard and the three Posse Men arrive at the BAT pulling up in front of Building C. Richard looks at his watch. It is at minute fifty-one.

"We have nine minutes," Richard calls out to the other three men. They get out of the cab and proceed to walk to the front door of Building C, which is unlocked. The night security team is likely out on rounds as the complex is technically closed. Lowenstein had unlocked the lobby doors.

From the shadows inside Building C, Lowenstein has noticed that Richard alone gets out of the cab with the three menacing, armed men, and no Hailey, so he knows the plan has really gone south and that he needs to make sure the escape route is set, and they carefully execute the escape plan.

"Shit, shit," he says. "No Hailey and three goons. Shit!" he says under his breath. Just as the three Posse Men and Richard enter the open lobby, Lowenstein kills the lobby lights from the master light switch panel in the rear of the lobby.

"What the fuck?" says Roger as the Posse Men spin around in the dark.

Richard knows he has to try to get some distance from the Posse Men, so while they look around in the dark for a light switch, Richard breaks free from his captor by leg sweeping him to the floor with a leg kick in the dark and runs in the direction of the back door. The Posse Man goes sprawling to the floor and the guns flies off in the dark.

Just then, Lowenstein appears in the back of the lobby near the rear door. He tosses the smoke bomb. It pours smoke all over the lobby. The Posse Men are startled and disoriented. Richard breaks into a run and is quickly out of sight. One of the Posse Men fires his gun, two shots in Richard's direction in the rear of the lobby but Roger stops him.

"Stop firing. We don't want the cops here. There have to be security guards around here somewhere. Go after them! He's got an accomplice!" yells Roger. "Here, take these flashlights!"

But Lowenstein knows there was only two roving night watchmen and the odds of them being in earshot are remote as they were out patrolling the other buildings on a sweep.

Roger knows Richard has to provide them the codes now, in less than seven minutes, assuming Richard is not bluffing, or he and his girl are both dead.

Lowenstein calls out, "Richard. I'm over here. We gotta hurry.

"Richard, you have to provide those account codes, or you and Hailey are both dead," calls out Roger. "You know you can't hide. We'll find you wherever you go. Come on, we don't have to do it this way. You only have like three or four minutes before Hailey dies."

Lowenstein sees Richard running towards him. "Richard, over here."

Richard and Brian meet up. "The boat is just over there. You gotta give these guys the new codes," says Lowenstein.

One of the other Posse Men says to Roger as they look for Richard, "Aren't we supposed to kill him anyway?"

Roger replies, "No, just bring him back with us. James wants him. We're not taking him to the airport."

"Fuck that. I'm going to kill that mothafucka."

Roger turns his gun on the Posse Man for effect. "You do that and you're dead. James still needs Richard."

Richard says hurriedly, "I need those codes, Brian, or they'll kill us both and Hailey."

Lowenstein says, "Dude, I'm sorry. Where's Hailey?"

"Simpson figured it out. I don't know how. Hailey's with him back at the Crack Den. Brian, I have like three minutes! If I don't give him the codes, he'll kill all of us. He gave me his word that he wouldn't kill Hailey if I give him the codes." Richard then removes the tiny laptop hard drive he wrapped in tin foil from between his butt cheeks and puts in his front pocket.

"Yo, man, that's too much information!" calls out Lowenstein. Lowenstein turns to Richard, "Yeah no problem, Richard. As soon as you got here and figured things went to shit, I called my connection in the Caymans on my satellite phone to cancel the transfers to the charities. And to transfer it back to the other holding accounts. Well, most of it. I still dispersed one million of the money. I'm a charitable guy. Anyway, I wrote the codes for the new accounts on a piece of paper and put it in an envelope and taped it to the inside of the third elevator in the lobby. Just let them know it's there."

"Shit! I have to run back there, so they hear me. Let's hope your charitable donations doesn't get Hailey killed," says Richard.

"Don't go too far. The boat is just behind this building," said Lowenstein. "I'll get the boat started."

"And oh, I made the donations in the name of James Simpson."

"Oh no. Now there's a trail!"

"Precisely, my friend."

Richard runs back to toward Building C and out of site, calls out to Roger when he is just in earshot range, "Roger, my old friend, I'm sorry it has come down to this. The codes are in an envelope, taped to the inside of the third elevator. Tell James I'm sorry. Please look after Hailey. It's not her fault." Richard then turns and runs back toward the pier and boards the powerboat Lowenstein has waiting and fired up.

The two Posse Men are pursuing Richard from about fifty yards behind when he jumps into the boat. They fire in the direction of the boat, but it is too far away from them.

Lowenstein races the engine to the motorboat, and they speed off into the night. Lowenstein, whose family is from Long Island, is an experienced boat operator. The Posse Men fire into the dark, not coming close to the escaping duo.

Roger runs to retrieve the envelope from the elevator, and opens it, and then calls Simpson on his satellite phone to relay the account codes to him.

"James, Richard got away. He must have had his escape plan all setup well in advance. He had outside help. I don't know how he planned it. But he did. Played us real good. He had someone cut the lights and throw some kind of a smoke bomb at us, while he escaped. His accomplice must have already taped the codes inside an elevator before we got there, and they got away in a boat. It was a good escape plan."

"Shit, shit, shit. All right give me those codes," says Simpson.

Simpson is standing next to one of the finance guys who punches the codes into the wire transfer computer program.

The accountant says, "The money's all here. Well, we're short a million."

Simpson growls, "Good. Short a million? Fuck. We'll I guess he needed a parachute. The fucker thinks of everything."

Speeding up the East River, Lowenstein says to Richard, "Where do you want to go now?"

Richard says, "Take me to JFK. I have to leave town. You have a satellite phone in this thing, right? Can I borrow your sat phone?"

"Yup."

SINFUL LOVE

Lowenstein hands Richard the satellite phone, and Richard calls Simpson in his office from the boat to again plead for Hailey's release.

"James, I gave you the codes. You got your money. I'm leaving town as you demanded. I'm going into hiding. Release Hailey. Please. You got what you want. Let us have a life. I'll never cross you, you know that," pleads Richard.

Simpson's parting words are, "You broke my heart. I trusted you. The only reason you're both not dead right now is that you made me a lot of money and helped make me richer. Remember my words. If I ever see you or get a hint you're in New York ever again, I'll find you and kill you *and* your girl. If you go and rat to the Feds, I'll waste Hailey. Have a nice life. I hope it was worth it. You won't be seeing your girl any time soon, maybe never. I'll take real good care of her. She's quite a looker."

"James, James, you lay a hand on her."

"And you'll what? You'll fucking do what? Payback is a bitch is all I can say. Later." Simpson hangs up.

Richard hangs up the phone. He is visibly shaking. Simpson's words sting, and his mind races, figuring out what to do.

"Yo, Richard, you better get out of town fast. These guys aren't messing around, friend, they have guns," says Lowenstein, putting his arm around Richard's shoulder. "I'm so sorry, man. What the hell happened? What went wrong?"

Richard hugs Lowenstein. "Brian, thank you so much. You are literally a lifesaver. I don't know what happened. James figured it out. Someone must have tipped him off. I think it was his guy Roger. He must have overheard me and Hailey talking about getting away from the Crack Den at the twelve-step meeting that time. Somehow, he knew everything we were planning, maybe he was following me, but he didn't give it away when we did our dry run two days ago."

"What, you talked about your escape plan at a twelve-step meeting? Are you crazy?"

"Brian, I know, I know. It was at that twelve-step meeting where I realized I had to do something to get us out. Hailey was sober. She was pushing me because she wanted us to have a normal life together. And that meant outside the den. A normal life together! I wanted that too, desperately. And I fucked it all up."

"What are you going to do? You got to get out of town, man. I'm sure he's going to have his people looking for you all over the place at bus terminals, train stations, airports."

"I know, Brian. I can't just leave. I have to get Hailey out of there. I can't leave her behind like that. James never was going to let me go, either. That's why I knew we had to escape."

"Yo, Richard, you need to regroup man. Go somewhere and rethink this. What else do you have on this guy? Anything you can use against him now?"

"I have all my files, everything is on the hard drive I removed from the laptop. It's all my insurance. I was going to use it to ensure Hailey and my safety going forward after our getaway."

"Well, why don't you use that to negotiate her release from the Den?"

"Brian, it would incriminate me as well. Who but someone who worked there, managed the finances, everything, would have this information? Plus, there's ledger files on there with names and everything. And you don't negotiate immunity with the FBI."

"Then give it to me after you remove or redact any files with your name on them, I will anonymously turn it in to the FBI," Brian says. "I have a friend at the FBI who I can leak this to with no questions. He'll protect my identity. He's pretty smart, though. He'll eventually figure out who it came from—someone high up on the inside who I must know. I can try to hold him off, tell him someone gave it to me anonymously, but sooner than later they'll put two and two together and they're going to come for you, and you may have to testify or something, Richard. It won't be pretty."

"If it can free Hailey, it's worth it. Brian, whatever we do, we must make sure Hailey is rescued. If anything happens to her—"

"It's not worth it if you do twenty to twenty-five years in jail for racketeering. Think this through. You need to make sure nothing, no evidence, points to you. You have to disappear, like you don't exist. Put your apartment in someone else's name, change all your bills, put in a forwarding address to some post office box in Podunk. You have to disappear off the grid, man, and you need to get it done like tomorrow!"

"Not a bad idea, but first I need time to make a copy of all the files to another hard drive and then remove the files that would incriminate me. I will keep the original drive as my insurance. The FBI has data forensic guys now that can revive deleted files, recreate stuff, so I need to copy the files to a fresh drive so they can't do that. I need to be super careful. Brian, do you have a place I can hang out for a day or so, so I can get this done?"

"Look, we'll go out to my folks house out in Long Island in Northport. They're in Florida, so we can hole up there."

"I don't know, Brian. What if Simpson or the FBI figures out who you are and then who your parents are?"

"Don't worry about it. They can't trace the house to me. My father put it in one of his shell companies before his first divorce so my mom couldn't touch it."

"I didn't realize your parents were divorced."

"Yeah, my real mom was a bit of a sociopath. Tried to have my dad arrested. I was young. My stepmom is a much better fit. My mom moved to New Orleans years ago. I see her once or twice a year."

"I didn't actually know that. I don't think I could ever call my mom a sociopath. That's reserved for someone like Harvey Weinstein," says Richard.

"Yeah well, she was—is. OK then let's head out there instead of the airport. Do we have a car?"

"Your wish is my command. I parked it in the long-term parking lot and took a cab back to the BAT. Aren't you glad I'm good with this clandestine stuff?"

"Great, Brian, yeah I am glad. But you'll need to cover your tracks, too. You can't be seen harboring a fugitive once we spill the beans."

"I have some latex gloves for us to put on while you're at the house so you don't leave fingerprints. We'll be careful," says Lowenstein.

They pull into a pier by a commercial storage building on the airport property. Lowenstein ties up the boat. "There's a landing on the other side. I'll go get the car and back it up to the landing. You can wait here. I'll come back for the boat to run it over to the landing."

Richard again thanks his friend who runs up the road at the end of the parking lot and flags a cab on its way to the airport. Lowenstein barks to the driver, "Long-term parking, lot A, please."

HAILEY IS LEFT BEHIND

Hailey is escorted back to Simpson's office by the Posse Men. Simpson is still in a rage when he approaches her. He grabs her by the arm, slaps her across the face, and bellows, "You knew about this?" Hailey falls to the floor.

"No. Richard did this on his own. I didn't know, James." Hailey is still lying on the floor.

"Oh, where's your boyfriend now? He lied to me, tried to steal my money, and blackmail his way out? He's gone, bitch! Left you in the rear-view mirror. He's heading out of town before I kill both of yo' asses. Now you're mine, ho, and you're going to be staying as my personal guest for as long as I say so!"

Hailey is despondent, crying hysterically, "No, no!"

"Looks like your homeboy took his freedom and his life without you. I guess you wasn't nothing to him after all…'cept a nice piece of ass."

Hailey begins to cry softly then stiffens. "You're cruel, James. All we wanted was our freedom to go on with our lives. We made you enough money. You didn't have to do this. You run this place like the Mafia. Richard knew you'd never let us go. Probably kill us. So, excuse me if we didn't exactly keep you in the loop."

Simpson slaps Hailey again and pushes her to the ground. "Smart bitch. You're right. The only way you two would have left here together was in body bags!"

Richard's friend Roger steps in and says, "James, I believe her that Richard didn't tell her. He concocted this up himself, like I told you."

Hailey looks at Roger in disbelief. "Roger…you…you told James Richard was planning our escape? You're just as bad as he is!"

"Hailey, I'm sorry it worked out this way. Really, I am."

Hailey shoots Roger a steely look. "Fuck you!" she says and then fixes her gaze directly at James Simpson.

Simpson, disgusted, yells, "Get her out of here!"

Roger helps Hailey up and escorts her to Richard's old apartment in the Den. Hailey opens the door with the key, looks in, and collapses on the couch in tears.

"Get out!" she yells at Roger who closes the door behind him. Hailey then cries softly, painfully for what seems to her like an eternity. She then falls asleep on the couch, a nightmare likely to come. What will tomorrow bring she thinks as she drifts asleep.

POST GETAWAY

Richard waits for Brian Lowenstein who is driving the car around to the nearby landing to retrieve the boat. Then he walks around the building, over to Richard, who is lost in thought standing next to the boat.

"Hop in. I'm going to bring the boat around to the landing on the other side of the building." Lowenstein eases the boat around the corner of the landing and where he has the car with the boat trailer. He uses the hooks and the hydraulics to pull the boat onto the trailer hitch. After about fifteen minutes, the boat is on the trailer and Lowenstein is securing it.

"OK. Let's get going. We can take the backroads to stay out of the limelight. My parents have a separate garage big enough for the boat, so it will be out of sight."

An hour later, they are pulling into the long driveway into Lowenstein's parents' house. Brian opens the garage door to the huge boat house and pulls the car in.

"I'll disconnect the boat in the morning. Let's get something to eat."

They enter the house, and Lowenstein disconnects the alarm,

turns on the lights and heads straight to the kitchen. In the freezer are different types of meats. He pulls out a package of ground beef.

Richard has no appetite. He misses Hailey terribly and still cannot process what happened. What went wrong? He keeps asking himself. "I'm not hungry."

"Bro, you need to eat something. Don't punish yourself. You need to concentrate on what you still have to do. I'll make us some burgers."

Richard nods. "Do you have a computer or laptop here, Brian?"

"I think there might be one in the study. There's a Nobody Beats the Wiz electronics store in the next town. We can buy you one in the AM along with that additional hard drive."

"I'll also need to buy an external drive container so I can read the hard drive I took from the den on the new laptop to copy the files on the external hard drive for the FBI."

"You got it."

"I'm going to check out that computer or laptop while you're making dinner. I like cheeseburgers, by the way," says Richard.

"Onions and mushrooms?"

For a fleeting moment, Richard smiles, "Sure."

Richard sits down at the desk in the den and turns on their desktop computer. There is no login and password, and Windows 3.0 starts running. Richard launches the Netscape browser. He connects to the nearby dial up modem for Internet access. Soon, he is accessing his offshore accounts, logging on from his memory. After seeing all his money earned at the Den secure in his own accounts, close to four and a half million dollars, he sighs in relief. He now accesses his Den Hotmail email meistermoneyman@hotmail.com account that he used at the Den without detection.

The account is still open! Richard has always been very careful not to send potentially damning information via emails. Still, he has over twenty thousand emails in his account that he had setup for the Den use. In preparation for leaving the Den, he has deleted many thousands of emails already, especially any that referenced the Den or Den business banking accounts used for petty cash or operating funds. He has been careful not to use his Den email account for anything that referenced him by name. He notices no new email traffic in the account since 5:30 PM when he left.

Scanning each email in his Hotmail account, he is convinced there is nothing remaining that is self-incriminating. He needs to do this in the event the FBI ultimately comes calling on him with a warrant and questions him about that email account.

Lowenstein shows up and hovers over his shoulder. "Yeah, you need to cleanse that email account, man. Can't leave any traces that connect you to that crack operation. I like the name you use on the account, meistermoneyman@hotmail.com. Funny."

Richard smiles for just an instant. "Yeah. It's suitably generic even for the FBI, not to draw any conclusions. I'm just thinking, if the FBI raids the place, Hailey could get hurt in the crossfire."

"Chance you gotta take, bro. Life in there can't be too safe for her otherwise and if we do nothing."

"You're right. But if anything happens to her..."

"Just make your move. Chances are the FBI will look out for her. We'll give them a heads up she's there as a hostage."

Richard nods but frowns.

"Oh no. Don't even think about it. You can't be anywhere near that place, Richard, when the FBI raids it. You are not going to try to rescue her."

Richard nods, but Brian knows otherwise.

"Once I get access to my files on that hard drive tomorrow, the FBI should move pretty quickly once we send them enough of the files that are incriminating enough to get them to raid the place. You have a nontraceable email account, right? I just need to know, Brian, that Hailey gets out OK."

Brian says, "Yeah, there's a library in town that has computers. I'll use their email account. The FBI won't be able to trace it. I know the librarian. I can charm her. Burgers are ready. You hungry? I am!"

The next morning, Brian disconnects the boat and trailer from the car before Richard arises. By 9:00 AM, they are ready to make their journey to buy a laptop and the other accessories in the next town over, and they can have the store's PC service department copy the document files from Richard's laptop to the new laptop's hard drive to save time.

Back at the house, Richard boots up the new laptop with the external hard drive enclosure and reviews all the files that were copied onto the laptop's hard disk so he can create a single folder and copy the files to the external hard drive they eventually plan to send to the FBI. The first wave of documents will be attachments in the email Lowenstein sends.

Richard has spreadsheet records of thousands of drug transactions, names and locations of the entire Den distribution chain, electronic records of all cash salary payouts to employees as well as the information on the offshore accounts where the money is stashed. Richard also has a record of all police, judges, and politicians who were on the payroll, albeit with coded names. All in all, Richard has tremendously incriminating information about the entire enterprise that he smartly, discreetly acquired in the last weeks there, a treasure trove of evidence.

Richard just has an epiphany. "Brian. What if I called James and told him I will turn over the hard drive to the FBI unless he releases Hailey? He's got to have figured out by now I have it. All he has to do is try to boot up the laptop. Without the hard drive, nada."

"You do realize if you play that hand, there's no turning back. If he doesn't bite or if he threatens to kill Hailey anyway, then he knows you're going to turn him in and you're a marked man for the rest of your life. If we do this clandestinely, we can warn the Feds there are civilians in there being held hostage—Hailey, the Home Girls—and tell them to treat it like a hostage situation. Leave James alone."

Richard realizes his friend was right. He really did want to get back at James for what he put Hailey and him through. Poor Hailey.

Oh my God. What's happening to her? Suddenly, Richard doubles over in pain at the thought. He was soon retching in his misery.

PLANS BACK AT THE DEN

Back at the Den, James Simpson nervously strides back and forth in his office. "Did you burn the fucking laptop from that turncoat?" he asks one of his enforcers.

"Yeah, we did. Watched it melt. All of his stuff was on the network anyway, so we didn't need it."

"Bring that bitch Hailey to me now! Strip her of her job and duties. Put her back in Home Girl circulation. I want that bitch high on crack! Forcibly if necessary. All day and night smoking that shit! Y'all can take turns with her."

Roger says, "James, Hailey didn't do anything. Look, you know I helped her get clean. She knows everything about the business Richard does. She's a real asset to us. Why do you want to throw that all away? Getting her high again, man, after she got clean, that's really cruel and it doesn't make sense."

James stomps over to Roger and smacks him in the face and says, "If you weren't so fucking soft on those two, I wouldn't be in the predicament I'm in! That fuck can ruin me if he rats to the Feds."

"He won't do that as long as he would be implicating himself and you're holding Hailey James, he won't rat on you. Hailey won't either. Why don't you let her go then?"

"Are you out of your fucking mind? You better be real wise right about now or I'm going to bust you down to the regular workforce and you can be packing the vials and shit," yells James.

Roger backs off, knowing that James is not in a reachable, reasonable place at that moment and may not be again for some time.

"Get that bitch high *now*. I want her on a binge until I say stop. I don't give a fuck if she vapor-locks. Do it or do I have to ask twice?"

Roger motions to John, one of the other Posse Men in the room, standing guard, and mumbles, "Do it."

James's rage subsides for a moment, though, walks over to Roger, puts his arm around him, taps him on the cheek that he slapped, and says, "Loyalty, man. It's time to step up and show your true colors."

"James, I have always given you my loyalty. It was me who tipped you off about Richard's plans. But I also give you my insights because I'm looking out for you. I'm asking you, don't do this to Hailey. She doesn't deserve it."

James laughs and says, "College boy, fucking college boy, just like your friend Graf. Got a soft spot for these useless bitches."

"Richard looked out for you, too. I know he made a big mistake, but come on, he made you tens—no, hundreds of millions. The guy is a genius with investments."

James waves Roger away and goes and sits down at his desk. "Yo, we're going to need to move our operations and fast. Too risky here after what happened with that punk Graf. We need to move the entire operation to Jamaica. Plenty of room there to lower our profile until we look for a replacement location back in Harlem or uptown."

"But, James, thanks to Richard and Hailey, we finally got the tenants on our side. We got the police in our pockets, looking the other way. Everything is just the way we want it."

"Yo, I know, but I got a feeling something is up. Call it a fucking gut feeling, you dig? Can't trust Graf. Start preparing. Do what you got to do from an IT perspective or whatever. Make sure everything is backed up on the servers and shit. Then remove all of them hard drives from everybody's workstations. Burn and destroy them. Take all them the new laptops Graf had me buy. Then get a team over to Jamaica and get things set up and ready to roll over there. I want this done by the end of the week. I don't want any evidence left behind after Friday. Get to shredding all the paper tonight. Get *everybody* on it. Buy a bunch of shredders, I don't care. Bag all the empty vials and shit. You know what to do."

"By Friday? Richard that's impossible. That's only three days from now."

"Yeah, by Friday. We had a good run here. After we close up tonight, get all the receipts and shit recorded and the accounts updated, shut things down for good, and we'll start our move starting first thing in the AM. You got until Friday morning, no later. After that, we're at risk. Don't make me go emperor from *Star Wars* and shit on you!"

"James, we're probably going to be leaving a lot of stuff behind, man. And most of these people preparing and cutting the crack are from around here. They're not going to go to Jamaica."

"Then we'll leave 'em behind! If they want a job, they'll go to Jamaica. If not, tell them they know what we do to disloyal employees. They'll get the message. Just make sure my runners are ready to roll. Don't want my youngsters left holding the bag." Roger nods. He has his work cut out for him.

THE FBI

Wednesday morning, Richard and Lowenstein are at the tiny library in Northport, sitting in the rear. Besides the young librarian no one else is around. They are at one of the PCs used for searching for books that has the Internet, a browser, and an AOL email program.

Lowenstein sweet talks the young woman at the library counter to borrow her phone. Richard is nearby.

"Sorry, I just need to call my mom to let her know I'm running late. Thanks. Oh, and I'll need the email password. I have to send her some information on her new medication."

The young woman is all obliging when Lowenstein bats his eyes and smiles.

Using the FBI's 800 number, Lowenstein reaches his connection at the FBI, Special Agent Narcotics Jeff Walker, with whom Lowenstein went to college. Lowenstein disguises his voice, "Can I speak to Agent Walker? I have critical information on a crime that's being committed involving drugs." Lowenstein is connected. He takes a deep breath.

"Agent Walker...who's this?"

"I have information and evidence on one of the largest crack operations in Manhattan, enough to put away the whole ring," says Lowenstein.

SINFUL LOVE

Richard looks at him awkwardly as Lowenstein has disguised his voice like Mickey Mouse. Richard shakes his head.

"Yeah, and I'm Mother Teresa. Who is this?" barks Walker.

Lowenstein changes his voice to sound more mature. "The information, the evidence is about James Simpson. Now I know you know who that is. His entire operation. I'm going to send an encrypted zip file to the FBI whistleblower email account if you don't believe me."

"No, send it to me at this email address. Who is this?"

"A friend. Give my love to Marcy," says Lowenstein and hangs up.

"Give my love to Marcy?" Richard asks.

"That's his wife. I figure he'll figure out it's someone who knows him. Just not me, hopefully."

Richard says, "Did he buy it?"

"Yeah, he did. He gave me his personal email account during the call. I wrote it down."

"OK. Let's do this," says Richard. They make their way back to the PC at the rear of the room. Richard pulls out two floppy diskettes, each containing a zip file with a directory of all the incriminating evidence of the Den operations. Enough to get the FBI started with indictments for sure until the copy of Richard's hard drive they plan to send arrives at the FBI. Lowenstein opens the library's AOL account enters the password and creates an email to Agent Walker and uploads the two zip files from the floppy diskettes.

"This should be enough to whet their appetite. I'll drop the hard drive off there this afternoon," says Lowenstein.

"Agent Walker," he writes in the email body. "Here is some information/evidence you'll need on James Simpson's entire crack operation including transactions, names, accounts, and even where the money is offshored. There's a lot more where this came from. One more thing: there are civilians, all women, being held hostage as sex slaves that need to be rescued, about twenty women. The address of the operation is 169 W 126 St. They are all on the fifteenth floor of the A building, all wings of the complex," writes Lowenstein. He hits the send button then high-fives Richard. Richard's heart is racing. Now what?

Lowenstein says, "You know, I didn't mention Hailey by name, man, because I was afraid that would give us, you, away."

Richard nods.

～

AGENT WALKER RECEIVES the email and looks at the zipped files sent by Lowenstein.

"Holy shit!" he exclaims and immediately calls the drug enforcement task force that has been working with NYPD to sting crack operations. Walker calls a meeting for later that afternoon after sending the information to the drug enforcement analyst team. He reaches out to the agent in charge to offer his help.

"This is Special Agent Walker in Narcotics. We got a hot lead on a major crack production operation up in Harlem—James Simpson's ring—that has a possible hostage situation. Let's work together. I've sent you and your team all the data that was sent to me anonymously. You'll want to get your analysts on this right away."

The head of the FBI's anti-drug taskforce replies, "Great. Just what we've been waiting for. We have some limited intel on Simpson. Thanks to this intel, we now know he has cops on his payroll, even judges, so we need to move carefully. I'll get my team together. Meet me in two hours."

And the charge is on.

The next day at FBI headquarters in New York, the FBI anti-drug taskforce leader is holding court in his situation room with his entire team surrounding him, field agents, analysts, his technical virtuosos, and monitors filled with data, FBI profiles, and footage of the Den itself.

"We finally got both the internal and evidence against this gangster James Simpson. Enough to put him away for a lifetime. Murders, extortion, racketeering, you name it. Where's our field agent lead. What's the attack plan?"

A top FBI field agent and team leader was ready to lead the actual raid on the Den at 0800 hours. The FBI has secured a warrant from a federal judge. They were only waiting on getting field agents and the team assigned and briefed. That was going to take place the remainder of the evening.

The field agent lead said, "We go in tomorrow, at 0800. Grab everything and everybody. We will have snipers trained on all four corners of the building. A preliminary team will go in first at 0700 to assess the hostage situation, gathering intel before we go in in force at 0800. We need to make sure we get the hostages out of there in one piece in case things get rough. They probably have a lot of firepower, and might use the hostages as their escape route. We have to neutralize their upper hand in holding of the hostages and take them by surprise. The brief in front of you contains details of the attack plan. Read it over and now's the time for any questions. You'll get with your teams later this evening to go over this as they arrive."

"I have the NYPD SWAT Team on the line. SWAT, you and your team will provide the sharpshooters and set up a perimeter and then be part of the secondary attack force once we have the hostage intel. You guys ready?"

"Absolutely," came the reply in typical SWAT swagger. "We got your back, and we're ready to take it down!"

When the long briefing had ended, it was close to 10:00 PM and the FBI Field leader closed with, "Rest up. everybody be here at 0500. We leave at 0600 for the complex in Harlem. Get our intelligence together at 0700 and be ready to execute at 0800 or before. Nobody in this room talks to anybody. Got that?"

BY THE END OF THURSDAY, the Den has finished packing of all of the computer servers from Harlem to the Jamaica location, removed most of the workstations' hard drives, and then destroyed the workstations, shredded most of the paper files and records with the plan for a skeleton team to finish up the following day. They have rolled a box truck out of there with all the surviving furniture, chairs, and other fixtures they will need in Jamaica as well as all the laptops Richard had told James to buy in order to be more mobile.

Each Posse Man is responsible for packing their own bags and equipment to bring with them to the new complex in Jamaica, same for the live-in accounting personnel. Richard's accounting team oversees the network take down of all the computer equipment and how it was loaded into the truck.

"Good to go," they say after everything is packed and labelled for transfer to the Jamaica location. The truck leaves for the Jamaica location just after 8:00 PM. They take as many passengers as they could fit.

The other employees who cook, pack, and process the crack and who also live at the Den, are soon to be told that they will report to the new Jamaica location for work. Fear for their lives keeps these employees loyal. All of the Crack Den employees are gathered together by the Posse Man leader Mookie in the elevator lobby at 8:00 PM for the briefing.

"That's right, everybody will pack into a school bus we've rented and will leave for Jamaica tonight. Be in the elevator lobby at half past 8:00 PM—that's thirty minutes from now—and you will be escorted downstairs to the front of the building. Don't be late or missing. We'll find you and you don't want that to happen," barks Posse Man leader Mookie.

"Apartment assignments will be provided for all the workers at the new living quarters when you arrive there. Don't be late or you will be dead!" Mookie continued.

The plan is for everybody remaining to spend a last night at the Den and then head out to the new Jamaica location after breakfast at 0900 AM. The plan does not include bringing the Home Girls along. They have no idea they are to be collateral damage, released into the streets in the morning.

SINFUL LOVE

Hailey has spent much of today and the days before forced to constantly get high with the other Home Girls. At all other times, she has been detained in Simpson's own private apartment under lock and key.

∼

AT 0600 AM the FBI's field ops, attack team and the SWAT team leaves FBI Headquarters at Twenty-Six Federal Plaza for the Den complex in Harlem. They arrive shortly after 0630 AM. The first SWAT team gather themselves in position. At 0700 AM, SWAT team members scale down from the roof to the fifteenth floor using ropes to enter the main building from a window by the fire escape on the fifteenth floor of the north wing. They have spotted the open window from the street. But the curtains are drawn so they cannot see inside.

Using infrared head gear, they immediately identify where the bodies are concentrated on the floor. But they are surprised that there is not more foot traffic. Maybe thirty people, no more. They wonder where all the drug workers and kidnap victims are. The FBI is expecting up to 100 figures for an operation of this size.

The trio of SWAT agents stealthily make their way from apartment to apartment on the north wing, searching for the Home Girls. They know they can only go so far without tipping off the rest of the Den workers on the floor. They determine from the files they received anonymously from Lowenstein that the Home Girls have been "herded" into several apartments on the fifteenth floor.

Finally, they come to apartment 15P, about a third of the way down the west hallway, and seeing six heat signatures, a female SWAT Agent opens the unlocked door, and the SWAT team shines the light on six Home Girls, appearing to be stoned or high. They squeal.

The SWAT leader whispers, "*Shhh*. We're going to get you out of here, but you must be quiet *now*."

"How many more of you are there? What apartment number?"

"They're in 15D on the other side of the building, the east wing, I think. About ten more girls, 15E, F, and G. Oh, and the white boy's bitch. She's in with the boss man in the main crib. You'll never get her."

"Where's his unit?"

"All the way up front. He's got her in his office, Apartment A. It's heavily guarded."

The SWAT leader radios in, "We have six of the hostages located. We expect six more are on the other side of the building in another apartment we'll secure. But there is one hostage being held by Simpson himself under heavy guard. We can't risk that."

The FBI Field leader quickly says, "No, you secure the hostages, but do not, repeat, do not, engage any of the hostiles. If they see you, we've lost our surprise. Keep the girls quiet, too."

Just then, one of the Posse Men walks down the hallway to check out where the noise is coming from.

One of the Home Girls hears the footsteps and yells out from inside the apartment, "In here! It's the *police* or something."

The SWAT leader clasps his hand over the Home Girl's mouth, gets his hand bit, and the Home Girl calls out again. The approaching Posse Man heard her call out and rushes to the room, alone, not calling for backup. He opens the door to find three SWAT members with their automatic weapons trained on him. As the Posse Man tries to make a break for the door, one FBI agent sweeps his feet out from under him and karate chops him to the throat, rendering him unconscious.

The FBI field leader outside has heard the action on his radio. "What the hell happened?"

"We had to take out one of the muscle guys. One of the hostages yelled when she heard him coming this way, and he must have heard her. But he came alone, and we've secured him."

"Yeah, but they will be missing him soon if they're paying attention. Does he have a two-way radio?"

"Negative."

"OK, that's good, so he couldn't have radioed for help, and they cannot contact him. That will buy us a little time. Time to mobilize."

"Give us about ten more minutes. We need to take more hostages on the other side of the building. I'll signal when they're secured."

"Roger," says the FBI field leader.

He hands the radio over to his superior, a senior FBI agent, who will now run the operations as the FBI field leader gathers his team. The plan is to enter the building from the rear and fan out into four teams, each with four members, with each team taking one staircase at each wing of the high-rise complex and then collapsing to the front of the building where most of the heat signatures were.

The SWAT leader in the north building calls in, "We've secured all hostages except for one and are escorting them out of the fire escape. The other hostage is with a hostile. You will have to neutralize him. He's in Apartment 15A. SWAT Team Leader out."

Each team makes it up the stairs undetected and then fans out through the four wings of the fifteenth floor. As they make their way forward, one of the teams encounters two Posse Men outside apartment 15C, they engage in gunfire and one FBI agent and both Posse Men are down.

James Simpson hears the gunfire from his office in Apartment 15A, bolts out from his desk, grabs his paraphernalia and gun, and runs out the door to the office into the apartment's hallway.

"James, we've been raided. I think it's the FBI. We gotta get you outta here," says Homer, one of the Posse Men who meets Simpson in the hallway, gently grabbing him by the arm.

"Motherfucker! Graf! Get the bitch," blurts out Simpson to the two bodyguards.

The Posse Men run to Simpson's private bedroom in the office apartment and find Hailey, drugged out, woozy, and lying on the couch.

"Let's go *now*," says one of the Posse Men, tugging at Hailey's arm. When Hailey remains motionless, the Posse Man picks her up like a sack of potatoes and carries her out on his shoulder. He meets Simpson, and they race for the fire stairs on the west wing of the building complex.

Then on the ninth floor, from the staircase landing, they take a detour through a hidden door and go down a private staircase that was added to the building just for Simpson to make quick getaways. He has an answer for everything. The stairs empty into an underground corridor that runs under the street—dark, dingy, and wet—and opens to a manhole cover a block down from the Den building complex on 127th Street. Simpson, the two henchman, and Hailey escape to the street. Not far behind them is Roger, who has trailed them the entire route. He catches up with Simpson. It is dark outside with huge thunderclouds almost making it appear to be evening.

"James!"

"Yo!" Simpson called back.

∼

ACROSS THE STREET, Richard and Lowenstein are hiding behind two phone booths and are stunned to see Simpson, Hailey, Roger, and the two bodyguards, one of them trailing and leading Hailey by the arm down the street in their direction. Hailey now seems coherent. By sheer dumb luck, Richard and Ben have staked out the Den from a block away because they know they cannot get any closer with all the police, FBI agents. They never figured that they would be in the right place at the right time.

"I'm so glad I let you talk me into this!" whispers Lowenstein.

"I have to do something!" says Richard, visibly agitated as he spies the Posse Men, James and Hailey coming toward them. There is a large black SUV on the corner of 127th Street, a block away from the den complex, the group is clearly headed toward. It is literally across the street from Lowenstein and Richard are hiding.

"Richard, no!" yells Lowenstein as Richard emerges from behind the phone booth and sprints across the street and lunges at the Posse

Man who has Hailey. The Posse Man lets go of Hailey, anticipating the collision.

Richard knocks the Posse Man over. Richard calls out, "Hailey, run!"

Hailey, startled but now fully lucid, takes advantage of her momentary diversion and freedom and starts to run. She never looks back to see who the attacker was. She did not recognize Richard's voice, either. She darts across AC Powell Boulevard past where Lowenstein is hiding and runs into the night and is soon out of sight before the other Posse Men or Simpson who are in the SUV know what has happened.

One of the Posse Men is about to pull a gun and shoot at Hailey's direction in the distance, but Roger grabs the barrel and pushes it toward the ground.

The other Posse Man strikes Richard with a punch across the face knocking Richard backward. He hits Richard again on the way down. Richard blocks another blow and sweep kicks the Posse Man's feet out from underneath him as he tumbles to the ground.

Simpson, now out of the SUV, is about to pull his weapon on Richard when he hears, "Halt!" loudly from a distance, close enough to make out the policeman and his revolver out. Too close! James hesitates to shoot Richard. Richard instinctively rolls out over and away from the SUV.

The commotion has already caught the attention of other police nearby who come running in the direction of the fracas with their guns out and flashlights blaring screaming through a megaphone, "Put down your weapons and surrender!" they yell and start firing their weapons in the direction of the SUV.

Two police cars are streaming up the avenue in their direction.

"James, we need to get out of here *now*. Now, James!" yells Roger. Simpson pantomimes shooting Richard after holstering his weapon, saying to the fallen man, "Another day, bitch."

Simpson and the two Posse Men jump in the black SUV and speed away into the night, heading uptown on AC Powell Boulevard where they make a fast right on 129th Street. Soon, they are across the Willis Avenue Bridge and take to the local streets in the Bronx.

Richard falls back to the ground, unconscious. The police trail them in the cars but lose the SUV.

Lowenstein arrives a few minutes later to the scene to check on Richard. "Richard, are you OK?"

The police arrive on the scene.

"Put your hands up!" they bark at Lowenstein.

"Don't shoot! I was only helping my friend. It looks like he got hit pretty good trying to help that girl out. It looked like they were trying to kidnap her or something. She ran off down 127th Street on the other side of the boulevard. I didn't see where she went after that," said Lowenstein. "My friend here like saved her life or something. Those guys had guns. But the girl got away."

THE HOSPITAL

Richard is being treated at the hospital where the police are interviewing him.

"I never saw them before tonight. I was standing on the street corner, making a call on the payphone, and I looked over and it looked like they were like kidnapping this woman, so I walked toward them to confront them when one of them suckers punched me a couple of times, and that's all I remember. I was coming out of the B Lounge with my friend Brian. I just had a few beers with him. I think she got away. I didn't see where she went as they were kicking my ass."

Being interviewed separately in another room, Lowenstein indicated to police that he never saw anything, that he and his friend both thought it looked like a kidnapping as the woman was clearly being dragged towards the SUV against her will. So, Richard tried to intervene. They were not aware the kidnappers were armed he said.

Richard asks patrolman, Harris, "What happened? Did the woman get away? I heard police coming in the background, so I was hoping you'd get there in time."

Harris says, "We didn't really see where the woman got away to. We looked, but we couldn't find her. Guess she's gone with the wind.

The men in the SUV got away, too. They fit the description of some criminals who were about to be arrested in an FBI raid in the apartment complex. Let me show you some pictures of this guy and his known accomplices and let me know if you recognize anyone who you say was trying to kidnap the woman."

Richard, looking down, composes himself, taking a deep breath because he knows he has to be convincing that he cannot identify Simpson or any of the Posse Men he escaped with or Roger. "It was really dark, and it all happened so fast. I couldn't really see their faces."

"Was this guy one of them?" Harris shows mugshots of Simpson, Homer, and Roger.

"I can't tell for sure. Possibly. Again, it was dark, and I didn't get a good look at anyone because they sucker-punched me and I blacked out."

Harris says, "OK, if you remember anything, anything, here's my card, call me." Harris hands Richard his business card. Richard nods.

Richard hides his concern that Simpson got away and that Richard realizes he needs to get somewhere safe quickly and then get out of town fast and cover his tracks. He knows it will not be safe for him in New York, no matter where Simpson is because Simpson will figure out it was Richard who notified the FBI and provided them with intel on his operation and then, no doubt, will retaliate against Richard once he finds him.

With police on his payroll, that should not be too difficult, Richard thinks.

But where is Hailey? He is relieved that in the scuffle that he somehow managed to help Hailey escape into the New York night. But now he is worried even more. Richard had noticed that Hailey did not look well, and Richard recognized right away that she must have been using again.

"Thank you, Officer. If there are no more questions, I'd like to get some rest."

"No problem. Thanks for your help. You're free to go." The two patrolmen left the hospital room.

SINFUL LOVE

Just then Brian entered the hospital room. "Hey, dude. How're you doing? How's your head?"

"I'm fine, Brian. What happened to you?"

"The police took me downtown to take my statement, but I just told them from where I was standing across the street, it looked like they were trying to force a woman into the car, and then I saw you, like a crazy man, go to try to help her. I said I came running after you, but they had punched you down to the ground, and before I got there, then they sped off uptown. I think they turned on One Hundred and Twenty-Ninth Street to go east. Richard, I didn't tell them I saw Hailey run across One Hundred and Twenty-Eighth Street into an alley, and I'm sure she got away because I lost sight of her real fast. Girl can really run! They couldn't go after her. The police came seconds later and wanted me to go to the precinct after I made sure you were in the ambulance headed to the hospital."

"Brian, where did she go? I have to find her."

"Dude, you have to get out of town and fast. I overheard Simpson say he was going to kill you before he took off. He was *really* pissed you helped Hailey escape."

"Brian, you have to do me a favor. You have to check all the hospitals and see if Hailey checked herself in. I need to know if she's all right. Can you do that for me? You have to find her!"

"Richard, if your girl is every bit as smart as you say she is, she's not going to check herself into a hospital because Simpson's going to be looking for her too, and you said he has cops on his payroll. She would be smart to lay low, and I'll bet she'll be getting out of town too, probably by bus or train, not by plane. Someway that is untraceable, you know, where you pay cash, and they don't take your name."

"You're right," sighed Richard. He recalled Hailey telling him she was a track athlete in high school and college which apparently did her service in running away swiftly from Simpson, drugs or no drugs. But there was a pit in his stomach because as he was being punched out by the Posse Men, he knew Hailey did not know it was him that helped her escape as her back was turned to him.

Lowenstein says, "Look I'll rent your place for you long-term now. We both know people looking for a place to sublet, and they can afford your place because it's rent-stabilized. Do you have someplace you can go to, like out of state, someone you can contact? You need to lay low for like years!"

Richard says, "Yeah, I do. I've been meaning to look up an old friend out west. I'll call him. Better you don't know who or where. I'll reach out when I'm safe." Richard turns to Brian and hugs him.

"How will I reach you, Richard?"

"I'll call you, Brian. At home. Help me pack so I can get out of here."

"Shit, I just remembered, I need to go to my apartment for some stuff. My passport, I have some cash there, clothes," says Richard through his fogginess.

"No man, you can't do that. I have your keys. Just tell me where everything is you need. I'll stuff it into a suitcase. Meet me at Ninety-Fifth Street and Third Avenue in the pizza place on the northeast corner at midnight. Meet me inside by the jukebox. I'll drive you to the airport. You better pay cash for your ticket wherever you're going. Don't use credit cards. They can track them. You also better get your hands on some cash, brother," says Lowenstein.

"Don't worry. I'm way ahead of you," says Richard, brandishing his ATM card. Before he had left the Den, Richard had made several cash transfers from his offshore accounts to his local Manufacturers Hanover Trust bank account, all under than the IRS red flag amount of ten thousand dollars to escape detection. This he had figured would be enough to cover his and Hailey's escape and to start over together.

It is bittersweet that he has to do so without Hailey. But somehow, he knows he will find her, maybe not today, maybe not tomorrow, but someday and they would be together for the rest of their lives. Richard chuckled as he thought this, envisioning Humphrey Bogart uttering similar words to his beloved Ilsa, Ingrid Bergman, as he sends her away to safety on a departing flight at the Casablanca airport in Richard's favorite movie *Casablanca's* famous last scene.

Would that repeat for Richard? Would he and Hailey someday be together for good?

GET OUT OF TOWN

Hailey is panting, her eyes glazed and dilated. She is walking her way downtown on Broadway, peering left and right in true paranoia and enters the M104 bus at 124th Street through the back door as it opens, pushing past passengers getting off who give her a stern look. She does not dare look back.

She gets off the bus at 112th Street and Broadway and stands outside John's Restaurant, a well-known diner that served Columbia students. Hailey had befriended the owner when she first came to New York City, visiting often. The owners, the Zachadoulis family, are always kind to her.

Hailey is hungry and needs a place she feels safe to come down from the drugs she has been forced to consume. She figures she can then go to nearby Columbia University. She still has her student ID card in her small purse she clings onto for dear life. Here goes nothing.

The son of the owner, Michael Zachadoulis, recognizes Hailey as she walks in. "Hi, Hailey. Hey, what happened to you?" He walks out from behind the counter to approach her.

"I was running with the wrong crowd. But now it's time to get my life back together. Michael, I need some food and to borrow your

SINFUL LOVE

phone. I can't pay you now, but you know I'm good for it. I will pay you back." Hailey barely makes eye contact.

Zachadoulis says, "Don't worry about it. It's good to see you though it's been a while." He hides the concern in his voice.

"Yeah, I got caught up in with some bad people, but I'm OK now. I'd love some eggs, some pancakes, and a cup of coffee." Hailey makes eye contact.

Zachadoulis offers Hailey a booth in the rear of the diner where she can have some privacy. It is just before eleven in the morning, and the diner is not as crowded as it is during the school day.

Hailey begins to feel nauseous, and she notices that this is the second or third day in a row that she has felt that way. While the drugs have masked it the past several days because she has not gotten high today, she is now coming down and gathering her clarity, and it is starting to come back. But she is also really feeling the need to get high. But she knows she has to fight it, knowing that eventually it will probably win. The recovery axioms return to her thoughts.

Hailey is starving and the breakfast tastes good. She has not eaten in days. The coffee tastes good, and she has several refills. She thinks about what to do next. She knows she needs to get out of town. She needs some money, and she needs help. Her mom's sister lives in Brooklyn. She was estranged from her mother, but family is family, Hailey figures.

Hailey asks Zachadoulis to borrow a phone book so she can look up her aunt's phone number. She knows she lives on Bedford Avenue. She is in luck and finds Anette Robinson on Bedford Avenue and dials the number.

"Hello? Aunt Anette? This is Hailey, your niece."

Her aunt's surprised but happy voice resonated through the receiver, "Hailey, so good to hear from you!"

"Hi. I'm actually in New York. I know it's been a long time. Yes, I know you and Mama had a falling out, I'm sorry about that. Aunt Anette, I really need your help. No, I'm not going to Columbia anymore, I dropped out. I kind of got caught up with the wrong crowd. Listen. I need your help. I need some money, some clothes, and a place to stay tonight until I can get out of town tomorrow. Do you have a car? Can you meet me at John's Restaurant on Broadway and One Hundred and Twelfth in the city right away?"

Hailey's aunt says, "I'll be there in about forty-five minutes. You stay at that restaurant until I get there." She hangs up the phone.

For the first time in a long time, Hailey feels a sigh of relief that maybe, just maybe, this nightmare is ending.

Forty-five minutes later, Hailey's aunt arrives in her 1990 Nissan Altima and parks right in front of the diner, putting her hazard lights on. She goes inside the diner, and Hailey immediately recognizes her and runs to greet her.

She looks back at Michael Zachadoulis and says, "Thank you. God bless you," Hailey embraces her aunt by the door and says, "We getter get going."

Just outside the door two black men walk stridently toward them and bump into Hailey and tug at her. "Hey, look at this little whore! I recognize her from uptown! Used to party! All you needed to do is give her a nickel bottle, and she would do anything for you!"

Hailey pushes back, but they have grabbed her by both arms and are dragging her off. But Zachadoulis has seen this through the diner's front window and comes running out. "Release her now, or I will call the police!"

Zachadoulis notices a police car streaming down Broadway a block away and runs out into the street to flag the police down. Seeing the oncoming police car, the two men drop Hailey on the pavement and run.

Hailey bounces up quickly and motions to her aunt to get in the car and tells her to start the engine. Two seconds later, they pull away and cross in front of the police car that is slowing down to cross over to the east side of Broadway to meet up with Zachadoulis and speeds away south on Broadway.

With a puzzled look, Zachadoulis turns around to see Hailey and her aunt drive away. He tells the police that the two men were threatening his customers outside of his diner, but they ran away.

The police officer says, "Did you get a good look at them?"

Zachadoulis says, "Yes and I've seen them before harassing people for money outside the restaurant."

"If they come back, call me. Can you come down to the station later today and look at some mug shots? " He hands Zachadoulis his business card as Zachadoulis nods his head.

Inside the car, Hailey cries softly. "I just want this nightmare to end."

"It's all right, dear. You're safe now from those horrible men. What did they mean by you liked to party and would do anything?" asks her aunt. Hailey just sits motionless and doesn't respond.

"It's nothing, Auntie, pay no attention to them," she finally says. Hailey just sits in the car, feeling safe for the first time in a long time. As they cross the Brooklyn Bridge, she smiles the further she gets away from her nightmare of the last several years.

THE TRAIN TO SOMEWHERE

Hailey spends the night at her aunt's and enjoys a good meal, a long, long hot shower, alone, for the first time, and a change of clothes. Her aunt has some clothes leftover from her own two daughters, who are about Hailey's size and away at college.

Hailey dials her best friend from high school LaShonda Okafur who lives in Chicago. She has not spoken to LaShondra since they were college seniors. LaShondra had gone to Northwestern and settled in Chicago after school and got her first job working as a political reporter for the *Chicago Tribune*. She is excited to hear Hailey's voice.

"Hailey! Oh my God! How are you? I'm so sorry we lost touch. I think about you often. I lost track of you these last couple of years. You're in New York, right? You were going to law school, Columbia?"

"Oh, LaShondra, I really screwed up. I got caught up in something really bad in New York. I…I…got addicted to crack cocaine. I need help. I also need to get out of New York urgently. There are some bad men looking for me. I didn't break any laws or anything. I'll tell you the whole story when I see you."

"Hailey, you get on the next bus or train here. I'll pick you up at the station. Just call me as soon as you get here. Oh, I'm so glad you called. I'll take care of everything, get you help. There's a really good clinic I know just outside Chicago. I'll take care of everything. I love you."

Hailey has to put the phone down for a second. The last time she heard those words was from Richard. "I love you too, LaShondra. I'm going to get good night's sleep and then take an early train tomorrow. There is an eight AM train that gets into Chicago like two AM tomorrow night. I know it's late."

"Hailey, I'll be there waiting."

"God bless you, LaShondra."

"Sleep well," says LaShondra.

The next morning, Hailey's aunt drives her to Penn Station to make the 8:00 AM train to Chicago. Hailey is wearing a baseball cap covering her eyes with her hair in a bun. She is wearing nondescript clothes. Her aunt drops her off on the opposite side of Eighth Avenue by the post office. Hailey is taking no chances in case Simpson's men are staking out the entrance to Amtrak on 31st or 33rd Street and Eighth Avenue. She crosses the street at 33rd, eyeballing the Penn Station entrance nervously. She sees a couple of homeless men standing outside the station, but she cannot see their faces.

She decides to continue to the 33rd Street Penn Station entrance and heads down the stairs. As she approaches the stairs, one of the homeless men reaches out for her.

"Hey, sweetie, got something for me?" he mumbles. It startles Hailey. For a second, she looks at the man dead in the face. Her heart freezes. But it is not someone from the Den. She turns her head and runs down the stairs to the concourse level.

She sees the big overhead train schedule sign grid with the departing and arriving train times. Penn Station is packed, mostly with commuters for the Boston or Washington, D.C. trains. Hailey spots that her 8:00 AM train was departing in twenty-five minutes from Track 3E. She needs to buy a ticket.

She makes her way to the ticket area and gets on the line with her head down the whole time. Then out of the corner of her eye, she spots a familiar face. It is Mookie! He is standing in the middle of concourse, rotating around as if looking for someone boarding one of the trains. Hailey gulps.

He's looking for me! Her heart races. *What if he looks this way? Stay cool. Stay the course,* she thinks.

Five minutes later, she purchases her train ticket with cash. Gate 3E is actually the gate at the far end and likely out of the range of Mookie's eyeshot. Hailey thinks she can board undetected. As she starts to make her way toward Gate 3E, the Posse Man almost as if by instinct makes his way from the opposite end toward Gates 3 and 4, which are directly opposite one another. The train for Gate 4 is going to Miami and is leaving at the same time as Hailey's train to Chicago at Gate 3. Mookie stops at Gate 3 and pauses there.

Hailey's heart races. It is now five minutes to boarding and the final boarding call announcement for the Chicago train has just occurred. People flock to the line and start moving down the escalator to the platform below, their tickets checked by the conductor.

Why hasn't boarding started yet for the Miami train?

Hailey freezes as she looks at the board above and sees the Miami train has not yet arrived from Boston. It is late.

For what seems like an eternity, Hailey waits in the shadows for five minutes hoping Mookie will give up. Then, as if by a miracle, with two minutes to spare, the overhead board updates the Miami train's departure time to 8:00 AM, and the announcement comes for boarding. Hordes of people make their way toward the line by the gate. This momentarily distracts Mookie, and he walks toward Gate 4 to inspect the line. Hailey makes her move, darting across the concourse, coming up literally ten feet behind him, flashes her ticket to the conductor, and runs down the escalator for Track 3 and never looks back.

When she gets to the platform with two minutes to spare, she still does not look back and boards one of the cars, walks through at least three cars, and then finds an inside seat on the right side of the train, away from the platform, excusing herself from the person sitting in

SINFUL LOVE

the outside seat. Still feeling paranoid, she slouches down in the seat, using the other passenger as cover.

She freezes when she sees Mookie stridently looking through the train windows on the platform side out of the corner of her eye. Her heart stops when he gets to the window that is directly across the train aisle from her seat. Mookie looks in, but Hailey is safely blocked by the other passenger and it is dark, and she ducks her head.

She sees him continue on to the next car and breathes a sigh of relief. Just then, the train pulls away from the station. Still slouching, she can see the Posse Man standing alone on the platform as the train pulls away, leaving him in the distance.

Hailey does not sit up in her seat until they are clearly out of Penn Station.

"Jealous boyfriend?" asks the passenger next to her, a smartly dressed white woman in her sixties, who smiles at Hailey.

"You have no idea," replies Hailey.

"Don't worry, dear. He didn't see you, I'm sure of that. He looked like a nasty man."

Hailey nods and then settles into her long train ride to Chicago.

The last several months flash before in her eyes. She sees the image of Richard when he says he was in love with her, when he held her and kissed her, followed by their last image together when Richard, after telling her he loved her, ran off leaving her behind at the Den caused her to tear up. Would they ever see each other again?

She remembers her faithful upbringing and whispers to herself, "If it is God's way and it is meant to be, we will find a way to be together some day." Hailey still loves Richard.

GOIN' WEST

Richard arrives at JFK airport, briefly hugs Brian Lowenstein, and enters Terminal 8, all the while carefully looking left and right for any of Simpson's men. He is wearing sunglasses, a dark navy-blue workout jumpsuit, a baseball cap, and a long black wig he had purchased some time ago as a Halloween prank. He looks unrecognizable, more like a rock star. Head down, he walks to the American Airlines counter and purchases a one-way ticket to Seattle, Washington, in cash. He notes the gate and proceeds toward security, carrying just a carry-on suitcase and duffle bag with him.

As he approaches security, he is relieved to not see anyone from the Posse. He removes his laptop under his watchful eye and places it in one of the buckets on the track. He waits on the line to go through security and soon becomes lost in his thoughts.

He is startled by a familiar voice, "Do you see that piece of shit anywhere?"

It is June Bug from the Posse talking to someone on a mobile phone! Richard is just two or three people away from the X-ray machines and passage through security, and his heart stops for a moment, but then looking straight ahead he proceeds to put his two bags on the belt. In the distance, he hears, "No, I don't see him. I know he's here somewhere."

Richard is stunned. How could the Posse Men have figured out he would be at JFK, much less Terminal 8 flying out?

He moves quickly through security and then on to his flight at Gate 23. Just to be sure, Richard does not linger at the gate until boarding time, instead wandering through the various stores and eateries to kill time before his flight. The forty minutes until boarding time seem like an eternity, but then Richard boards his flight and gets to his seat without incident. Richard is not sure how they tracked him to the airport and this terminal but for now he has dodged a bullet.

∽

Outside at the gate, the Posse Men are talking on a payphone, "Yeah, we know he was here. But we must have lost him. Too many people. Too much interference here."

"Well, then find out what flight he was on and where he went," snarls a familiar voice, James Simpson at the other end. "James, if he's as smart as you say he is, he probably used a fake ID and paid cash. We're not going to be able to find out what flight he was on," said Mookie.

Richard settles into his seat, the midday sun shining through his window. Soon, the flight taxis out to the runway and is in the air. Richard stares outside the window as his five-and-a-half-hour flight to a new life begins. He feels despair set in big time. The woman he loves is gone, probably hates him for leaving her behind to ensure his own escape, does not even realize it was Richard who risked his life and helped her escape from Simpson, and he isn't there to comfort her. The guilt is eating him alive. He eventually nods off as the plane roared onto Seattle to his new life.

Someday, they would reunite, Richard knew.

WELCOME

Welcome to Sinful Love: Finding Love in the Wrongest of Places, the first book in the Sinful Love series. If you enjoy stories about explosive interracial love in the most ardent of circumstances with heroes that find out what it really is to be heroic in love, you're in the right place! You'll also want to see how the story continues, so stay tuned for Book 2 in the Sinful Love Series.

If you would like to be notified when the next book launches, or any other stories in the series, sign up for our newsletter and follow me:

Newsletter signup:
subscriberpage.com/richardschreibermailinglist

www.richardschreiber.com

Email: richard@richardschreiber.com

Facebook: @RichardSchreiberAuthor
Twitter: @Richards_Author

ABOUT THE AUTHOR

Richard Schreiber is an American author born and raised in New York City. He lives with wife of 16 years, Margarita and their 14-year-old daughter Katarina. Richard is active in the autism community and is a strong proponent for diversity and inclusion in the world and a proud co-founder of the Ubuntu Initiative, creating the Ubuntu Game to teach diversity and inclusion on the scholastic level.

His passion for seeking multi-cultural experiences grounded in love inspired him to write his first romance novel and many more to come. His belief that we are stronger because of our differences in heritage, culture and expression are the foundations of his writing and the recipe for a greater more harmonious, accepting world.

I would love to hear about your stories of the love of your life, even if they proved elusive to you. I promise to honor you by telling your stories through my characters in future stories. Please email them to me at

richard@richardschreiber.com

THANK YOU

Thank you for Reading Sinful Love: Finding Love in the Wrongest of Places

I hope you enjoyed the book. It is the first book in a series of three books that traverse the world and love of these two characters and the sustaining power of unconditional love. I would love to hear what you have to say. I am always looking to get better in seeking the truth about love in my writing.

Please leave a review on Amazon if you're able to let me know what you thought of the book. As an indie author this really helps to reach new readers. I thank you again from the bottom of my heart for our support!

Richard Schreiber

ACKNOWLEDGMENTS

I would like to thank my wife for her inspiration in defining what is unconditional love and to ground my story with her love. The love I have for our cultural differences and their beauty give me a deeper appreciation for our love. I would also like to thank all the wonderful friends, acquaintances and loves in my life that also inspired me. I would also like to acknowledge the many leaders of diversity, too many to mention. Your strength and grace and yes even militance shaped my values that equality and justice should be inalienable rights for all.

I would also like to thank RE Vance for his incredible coaching, humor, encouragement and grace and for making the journey in writing both illuminating and purposeful. I also want to thank my editor Pam Elise Harris who stuck with me through the early ugly days and who helped sculp my book with immeasurable guidance, patience and heart. Without your contribution, this book would never have evolved into a finished product. Also, thanks to Diana Buidoso for her work designing our marvelous book cover.

And a special thanks to my mentor, friend and an awesome writer in his own right, Waldo Rodriguez, for his leadership, guidance, encouragement and knowledge, without whom this book wouldn't have happened.

I am most grateful and thankful to all.

Much love,

Richard

WANT TO READ MORE?

If you enjoy interracial romances and want to see what happens next with Richard Graf and Hailey Ross stay tuned for Book 2 of the Sinful Love Series. If you would like to be notified when the next book launches, or any other stories in the series, sign up for our newsletter and follow me:

Newsletter signup
subscriberpage.com/richardschreibermailinglist

www.richardschreiber.com

Email: richard@richardschreiber.com

Facebook: @RichardSchreiberAuthor
Twitter: @Richards_Author

Made in the USA
Coppell, TX
18 October 2022